THE TOY SOLDIER'S HEART

THE TOY SOLDIER'S HEART

by Charlie Hufford

CARTER PRESS

OAKLAND CALIFORNIA

Carter Press, P.O. Box 1136, Oakland CA 94604

Library of Congress Catalog Card Number: 92-75140
ISBN 0–9634913–9–3

FOR MY BROTHERS

Dave Hufford

J. E. Freeman

Randy Bennett

Joe Capetta

Rob Carter

I

This afternoon, a bright chilly afternoon in October, Kenneth Charles Cooper has run all the way up Academy Street, leaping the occasional puddle.

In his room, he dumps his schoolbooks on the floor ("K.C.," his mom is always telling him. "I don't for the life of me see why you have to drop things on the floor. You're seven years old. That's old enough to know better...") He turns on the radio and flops on the bed, eagerly opening the newest issue of Uncle Teddy's Storybook.

4

Uncle Teddy's Storybook is the best magazine in the world.

And The Toy Soldier's Heart *is the best serial* Uncle Teddy's Storybook *has ever printed.*

Biting a long strand of Sugar Daddy from the stick, K.C. turns to page twenty-seven:

"But I can no longer run in circles," said the little plastic mouse. "I lost my key and no one wants me anymore." The little mouse looked up at the toy soldier sadly. "No one wants a little mouse that can no longer run in circles."

"We will find you a key," said the toy soldier, taking his little friend, the mouse, into his strong though rusty arms. "Until then," said the toy soldier, "you may ride on my shoulders."

"If you will find me a key," said the little plastic mouse, "I will help you find your heart."

"I will call you Johnny," said the toy soldier, looking into the little mouse's deep brown eyes. "And you can call me Michael."

"Look," said Johnny. "There is a boy in a boat. He is waving to us."

"That is Gabriel, our boatman," said Michael, the toy soldier. "He will never grow older. He will always be small and sunburned and he will never go far from the water."

"And who are they?" Johnny asked, pointing his little gray nose at the two boys seated behind the little boatman.

"My name is Bobby," called the older boy. "I am the toy soldier's truest friend."

"And I," cried the younger boy as the paper boat glided across the lily pads, "am their brother in blue."

K.C. looks at the picture on page twenty-eight. Gosh, Uncle Teddy's Storybook *has some of the best artists in the world working for them. It's almost like you can reach out and touch the colors, they're that real. And the ink smells good, too. A little like finger paint. If you lick it, it even tastes a little like finger paint.*

"Thumbelina, Thumbelina, pretty little thing," sings the radio.

As the days grow shorter and the nights darker, K.C. dreams of the wonders from Uncle Teddy's Storybook. *And, as the days grow into months, and the years wander on, he dreams of other wonders.*

Time, too, works its wonders. K.C., wandering with it, will grow into other dreams. Brighter dreams. Bright as the angels named in them.

Sometimes we forget. We think that it was so much easier when we were children. We reinvent the past. And now, we travel through the Carpathian alps, armed against the night with crucifixes, holy water, and a Book of Common Prayer.

Perhaps K.C. has dreamed himself, a child happier than we have known, a young man nicer than we have been. The lover we only dreamed of. Later, he may die for our dream.

Some dreams are not for everyone.

SOLDIERS

"Just tell me when you need money," he has told the boy.

"But sometimes you forget." He looks at his feet. "It's embarrassing."

Michael can remember sitting on the toilet in his undershirt when he was a little kid. Sometimes he'd look between his legs and see his soldier hanging there, a little man with a pink helmet on his head.

He smiles. In the gray hangover light, he looks at the boy sleeping beside him.

The boy sighs and smacks his lips. "Did you park the car?" he murmurs from the depths of a shallow dream. He is painfully thin, huddled and pale with sleep.

There is a snapshot in a pigeonhole in the desk. It is slightly out of focus, its edges curled, its colors turning. The boy is leaping in the air, dark, wet hair flying around his laughing face, his thin, knobby legs suspended in a blur above uneven ground. Borrowed red bathing trunks several sizes too large for him slide low on his hips.

On his thirty-ninth birthday, Michael had thought of his Aunt Vivian. "Thirty-nine and holding. When they ask me, I always say 'Thirty-nine and holding.'" She would shake pink henna curls, fossilized in hairspray. "Ayuh. Thirty-nine and holding. Holding what I don't know," she always said. "But I'm holding."

Michael was now thirty-nine. And holding.

...

Johnny was twenty-four now. And he wouldn't go back. Not this time. This city was a lot easier than LA.

Behind the heavy crates, he shoved his sleeping bag and backpack into a corner. They were safe there until Monday. He knew the janitor's schedule. He chinned himself up on the shelves at the north wall of the basement and crawled out the jimmied window. Closing it carefully so it wouldn't latch, he stood at the foot of the concrete steps and brushed off his jeans.

The fog was in. He looked at the luminous dial of the watch on his thin wrist. Several hours before midnight. No need to rush. He cut across the small park, freshly mown grass wet beneath his Addidas. A vague shape ahead to the left paused. Ears like bats, he thought, and smiled. He knew that bats didn't have ears. Radar. It was like radar, the way they could hear you. Like they could hear the blood pounding in your veins.

"Cold night," the man said. A cocker spaniel, his excuse for a walk in the park, smelled the boy's trouser leg, wagging its stumpy tail.

...

It is shirt-sleeve weather. Michael turns the corner of 18th and Castro and finds himself on the weed-tangled shoulder of the road that leads down from Spafford to the lake. It is a still afternoon, dusty. In the distance, he can hear an outboard motor. Through the trees, he can catch glimpses of the sandbar and the boarded-up hotel beyond it. But the hotel isn't boarded up. Music from the jukebox sifts through the rusty window screens. He passes the dock and general store, the gasoline pumps and the Nehi sign with the busted thermometer on it. A little girl sits on the steps, dribbling a grape popsicle.

Down the road, he passes the Lindstrom's cottage.

Mr. Lindstrom is out mowing the side lawn. He nods to Michael, wiping sweat from his forehead, and his wife calls hello from the kitchen window. Although Michael knows the Lindstroms have been dead for more than a decade, he smiles and waves.

Around a bend in the narrow road, where the blackberry bushes meet in a tangle with the poison sumac, he stands looking down the gully at the fishing camp. Tire tracks lead past the lilac bushes to the side lawn. From the road, he can see the Nash, the Buick, and the Edsel, parked at the edge of the swamp.

The door is standing open between the twin silver beeches. The front room is streaming light. As he enters, he can smell the smoke of Uncle Vernon's endless cigars. It seems to hang in the room, swirling with the motes of dust in the filtered sunlight.

Aunt Vivian, in jeans, a flannel shirt, and an apron, stands in the kitchen doorway, souvenir sombreros hanging on the wall behind her. She is holding a frying pan.

"Come on," she says. "I've been expecting you. I made your favorite things. But come on and sit down because we don't have long."

Michael knows he shouldn't say anything about Vernon. Because Vernon is dead and talking about him might upset her. The fact that Vivian is dead as well seems to escape him completely.

"You know," Aunt Vivian says, passing him some frog legs, "I don't know where your friend is."

"Gabriel?" Michael says, scooping up some pan fries.

"Ayuh." She smiles and shakes her head. "Always liked him," she says, patting his knee. "But I want you to watch out," she says. "That boy isn't him, so don't make any mistakes about it, okay?" Michael nods.

...

Johnny watched the sleeping body beside him, its chest rising and falling, rising and falling. The creep had tried to kiss him. He is lying rolled up in a ball and he feels very small under the covers. He should check out the man's wallet and go now. But the bed is warm and large enough that he doesn't have to lie too close to the sleeping body. He yawns and, slightly sullen, jerks himself off. With a satisfied smile, he wipes his hands and belly on the silk sheets. He sleeps.

...

Shaving, Michael is surprised by the mirror. The phone rings.

It's a wrong number.

His last two clean socks don't match and all his underwear is dirty.

...

Late afternoon in the basement. Damp, gray light through the dusty panes of glass high in the stone walls. He sits Indian style on his sleeping bag, leafing through the latest issue of GQ. On the glossy page before him: a swimsuit advertisement. A young man with cellophaned hair, his face as expressionless as the lean, firm expanse of his expensive torso. Johnny hates him.

But he will love him in his huddled sleep when, naked, he will slide into the sleeping bag with him, flesh as hard and smooth as stone. They always come to his sleeping bag in the early morning hours, leaving phantom cars parked with motors running as smoothly as their whispered litanies of desire. "Johnny," they whisper, "we love you. Because you are beautiful." And their bodies couple with his. "You are one of us," they sigh, tears in their eyes as they come.

...

Michael popped open a beer and sat in the sagging armchair. He was due at Don's in less than an hour.

"If you go home with that kid," Bobby had said to Michael in the smoky haze of happy hour, "you'll miss Don's party."

"There's a party in his pants," Michael said. "And he wants me to come."

"Don't you ever get tired of being Mister Rogers?"

"He isn't that young."

"He's younger than me."

"Who isn't?" Michael grinned.

"You," Bobby deadpanned. Then he laughed. The room was loud around them. "I miss Baltimore," he added more softly.

"Baltimore was years ago," said Michael. "We're here now."

But it's not the same, Bobby thought.

"Can I get you another beer?" the kid asked, returning from the bathroom. He had the platinum hair of dead screen sirens and the dark roots of porno idols, very stoned green eyes, sulky lips, and a chipped front tooth. His clothes were faded blues, remarkable only for what they failed to conceal.

"Sure," Michael said.

"Maybe later," the kid said, "you can come over to my place and I'll sit on your face."

"I don't get it," Bobby said, dropping Michael off at his apartment building. "He'd of done anything you wanted and then some."

"Maybe," Michael said, "he's too much like you."

"See you at Don's," Bobby had said as Michael slipped out the passenger door into the darkening street.

An hour later:

The mirror catches Bobby naked, glistening wet from the shower, one arm reaching for a towel.

He's not like me, he whispers soundlessly to the mirror. He's not. His reflection turns slowly to face him in the full-length mirror.

Bobby thinks about the boy in faded blues that would have done anything for Michael. His reflection smiles. It's thinking: But you do look like him. And you're like him. At least in that way . . . About Michael.

Yes, Bobby whispers to the naked man in the glass.

He had dreamed of Baltimore again the night before. And Michael. And the youth Michael would not let go. Michael's own and that of others.

. . .

Johnny had met Blue one night at the Station and gone home with him because he was tired, crashing from some speed he'd gotten from a john. He'd fallen asleep while Blue was fucking him, his face lost in the pillows. They'd laughed about it in the morning. He ran into him every once in awhile on the street. They weren't really competition. Blue was tall and muscular and never took it up the ass. He did an act at a private club downtown and he had done a dozen films and videos. He only worked the streets for a goof.

One Friday night he ran into Blue on the Muni. He wasn't headed anywhere in particular, so when Blue told him there was a party in his building, he tagged along, knowing there would probably be food. He hadn't eaten since the day before.

"They're nice guys," Blue said on the way up the stairs. "Kind of straight arrow, but okay." He laughed. "Don gets a kick out of introducing me as their famous neighbor."

"What about me?" Johnny asked.

He winked. "Want me to say you're one of my tricks?"

He paused on the steps. "Naw," he said. "Just let me be who I want to be." He tucked in his shirttail.

"Who's that?" Blue laughed, ringing the buzzer.

"Fuck you," Johnny said as the door swung open.

…

Michael watches Johnny sleep. He has kicked the quilt back on his side of the bed. He is wearing a football jersey, now rumpled up around his hairless chest, a jockstrap, and one knee-length striped cotton sock. Michael smiles, knowing that the boy has decided that wearing such bits of clothing to bed is collegiate and, therefore, sexy.

When Michael was a child, four or five years old, he liked to dress as an Indian. He'd make a loincloth of one of his mother's tea towels and draw lines on his face with finger paint. Once he'd tried to make the lines with crayon, but finger paint was better. Then he would put on the feathered Chief Ticonderoga headdress that his Aunt Vivian had bought for him at the dime store. The dime store had a floor that smelled of creosote and it was dark and full of wonders.

He gets up quietly and checks his wallet, a morning ritual now, before grinding his coffee.

He watches Johnny's face, crushed and vacant on the rumpled pillow. His mouth is half open. His eyelids flicker briefly and he moans. Michael tries to picture him as a child of five. He tries to imagine him as a black and white snapshot fastened with little foil corners to the black pages of someone's album.

When he was five, Michael thinks, I was twenty. And Gabriel was already dead.

That night at Don's party, Johnny had walked over to him and introduced himself. "Hi," he'd said. "My name is Johnny Clay and I like older men."

Yes, Michael thinks now. Yes. And you hate them, too.

"Leave on the light," Johnny had said that night. "I want to see you," he had said, meaning: I want you to see me. With a grin, he had taken Michael's cock in his hand and made sounds like a car engine, twisting it this way and that, as if it were a stick shift.

...

He hadn't taken the lithium for over six months. Obviously, his body chemistry was changing. He hadn't had a really bad spell in weeks. And everything was looking up now. Johnny knew that Michael was fond of him. And he was fond of Michael, as well. That was why he had to make sure that Michael only knew the person he would be someday. When he was with Michael, he was that person.

He knew that things were going to get better now. He was actually getting well. He knew that he didn't really work at a recording studio south of Market. But he's been there with Blue. Blue knew all kinds of people. And someday maybe Blue could even help him get a job there. He had only told Michael about the job so that he would see that he was serious about a career in music.

But he wished he hadn't told Michael about his father. He hadn't really had to tell him. That was one of the things that worried him about Michael. He didn't ask him questions. It was easier when they asked you questions.

They usually asked the same questions. And all of them asked questions eventually. He knew that much.

It made him almost angry sometimes. If Michael didn't ask him questions, maybe he didn't really care. But Michael must care about him. He's given him keys. That's why he'd told him about his father. He'd told him that he'd just moved up from LA and had been staying with his father for a couple months until his new apartment was ready.

He never would have told Michael all those things about his father and the house and the cars if Michael had just asked him some questions. And about how they would spend a couple of nights a week in his new apartment once it was painted. Keys. Michael had given him keys. If Michael hadn't given him keys, he wouldn't have had to lie about his new apartment. But it really wasn't a lie. If he'd had an apartment . . .

It had given him a headache, worrying about it and about Michael not asking him any questions. So he told Michael that he had to work tonight.

The only light in the mirrored bedroom came from the television set:

"Don't," Johnny said, rolling onto his stomach. "I'm watching Perry."

"It's the commercial."

"But Perry will be back in just a minute," Johnny smiled. "Maybe later."

"Maybe now. You can still watch TV. Just spread your legs."

"Be nice," Johnny whined.

"Fifty bucks is nice enough. I don't know why I put up with you."

"Because I'm cute," Johnny whispered, spreading his legs and hugging the pillows.

"Oh yeah," the man groaned. "Yeah . . ."

"Shhh . . . The commercial's over. Look . . ." He giggled. "Look at Perry . . ."

Mentioning the fifty bucks! He watched Perry Mason and he didn't move a muscle. Treat me like meat, he thought, and that's what you get. Meat doesn't move. I'm cute, he thought. And you're not. Someday, he thought, someday, someone might do something awful to the cheap bastard. He wondered who the actress was on the stand now, being cross-examined by Perry Mason. Michael would know who she was. This fuck, he didn't even know his dick.

. . .

Michael hears music in his sleep. He turns his head on the pillow. He needn't open his eyes, he needn't even wake up. Through his closed lids, he can see Johnny sitting in the rattan chair, watching the television. Johnny is staring at the television intently. He is dressed in J.C. Penney's underpants. He is very small. His head, with its cowlicks of black hair, seems almost too large for his thin body. He is so small in the rattan chair. His skinny legs don't reach the floor.

Johnny is four years old. In the flickering light of the immense television, Michael can see that the boy has a black eye and there are four large bruises on his small arm.

The music on the television seems to grow stronger and fainter with the breeze. Johnny is staring at the screen. As if standing behind the child in the rattan chair, Michael can see the immense screen now:

The sandbar at the lake. The lapping water of the lake reflects the sunlight, turning it into shards of cold silver. The music, tinny and fragile, is floating across the cattails and rushes between the sandbar and the old hotel, three-minute dreams for a nickel. There, where the immense screen is growing wider, is the rowboat, flaking red paint. A boy stands in the boat suddenly and waves, dark, wet hair flying around his laughing face. Borrowed red bathing trunks several sizes too large for him slide low on his hips. The bathing trunks are Michael's.

Michael shouts for him and runs into the shallows. As he dives into the deeper water, he looks over his shoulder. Behind him, stretching from the horizon to the clouds, a patch of sky is missing. In the darkness there, the small, battered boy sits in his rattan chair, watching him intently. A small child that fills the sky . . .

"Guess what? Guess what?" Johnny laughed as he shook him awake. "Look," he said, crawling into bed with him. "I got us a bag of doughnuts." The radiator was clanking. The alarm would ring soon. The sandbar was gone. "I just got off work," Johnny said, smiling and spilling a bit of jelly onto the comforter. "Did you miss me?"

. . .

A bright place, all chrome and glass. Through the sliding glass doors, the pool blankly reflects the sky. Motionless young men with spiky hair lounge in brightly colored canvas-backed chairs, their golden flesh glistening with lightly scented oil and deodorized sweat. Some are naked, some wear clinging Speedos on which the price tags have not yet been removed.

Johnny yawns and rolls onto his back on the diving board where he has been sunning himself. Shielding his eyes with his right hand, he looks down the firm, deeply tanned expanse of his own naked flesh. The body of a god. He stretches long, graceful legs and sighs. He is even more beautiful than those surrounding him. Taller. More elegant. And wealthier. Wealthier, as well.

Leaning on one elbow, delighted with the sinewy play of muscles beneath his sun-bronzed skin, he looks at the young men around him.

In the blinding stillness, all the young men open their eyes at once. All eyes are on him as he stands slowly, smiling.

Behind him, in the pool . . .

He won't turn around. He stands, motionless, watching the beautiful young men. They are smiling now. But their smiles . . . He hears a whisper from the pool behind him and the sun turns blindly away. There are shadows crawling everywhere.

With a sickening lurch, the body he has been wearing is torn from him and he falls onto his hands and knees, small, pale, and frightened.

Johnny, the thing in the pool whispers. Come here, Johnny. The smiling young men stand at once, dissolving in their laughter, the light of the place dissolving with them, the warmth fading with their vanishing flesh.

He is lying on his side on Ohio floorboards. His underwear is torn.

"Now," the bloated thing that was once his stepfather says. "You gonna be nice or am I gonna have to make it rough?" It undoes stained overalls. "Up to you," it wheezes. "Nasty or nice."

He shivers against the rough wood. He is very small and miserable. He is missing one of his baby teeth. There is blood in his swollen mouth.

. . .

"Johnny?" Michael said from the doorway.

"Nice," Johnny mumbled from the depths of the comforter. "Be nice . . ." He sighed. His breathing became even again.

"Dreaming," Michael smiled, reaching for his jacket.

. . .

Johnny opened his eyes. The sheets on Michael's side of the bed were already cold. Fog pressed against the windows, drowning the room in grayish light.

In the breakfast nook, Michael had put out Johnny's Daffy Duck bowl and mug. Next to the box of cereal was a tin foil packet of cocoa. While he waited for the water to boil, Johnny took a crumpled piece of computer paper from the zippered pocket of his windbreaker.

VersaTeller 0357.

. . .

Numbers flew by on the microfilm reader-printer. Michael was on automatic pilot. Captain Video searching for the code numbers on old insurance claims. 095–46–8055–B10. Zap! Wet copy shot out of the slot. Now . . . Cruising for 544–98–6078–M14. The film swept by in negative on the dusty screen . . .

His line buzzed. The asteroid shower of numbers on the screen whirred to a full stop.

"Kingsley," he answered in a puff of smoke.

"Michael," Johnny's small voice whispered in the receiver. "Are you coming right home after work?"

"Sure," Michael smiled.

"We gotta talk," the small voice said.

"Is anything wrong?"

"I don't know," the boy murmured. "But we gotta talk."

"Kingsley?" the manager's voice cut in on the line. "Is this a personal call?"

...

Johnny had stood under the shower, hot water cascading over him, for almost an hour. He would have stood there even longer but the hot water had run out.

Clean, he had dried his hair carefully with the blow-dryer. Solemnly, he had examined his body in the steam shrouded mirror. His body depressed him. But he knew that others wanted it. Michael wanted it. The question was did Michael want it enough?

He had dressed carefully in his new 501's and red flannel shirt. The clothes hadn't cost very much because he had bought them in the boy's department at Macy's. He was small enough to do that. Boy's sizes were less expensive. There were always more sale items in the boy's department and the clothing was just as good as adult clothing. It looked the same, really. Just smaller.

He had set the table. The dishes didn't match, but that wasn't his fault. None of Michael's dishes matched. But he was going to cook dinner. He wasn't a great cook. He knew that. But he could prepare good, simple fare. He could show Michael that. He had unpacked the groceries. He had opened the package of hot dogs and put them in a pot full of water on the stove, ready to boil. He had put a can of pork and beans in a saucepan and laid out brand new bottles of ketchup and mustard. He had unwrapped the hot dog rolls and put them on a chipped blue plate on the table. He had put potato chips in a large salad bowl.

He had sat in the rattan chair. But he hadn't turned on the television. He hadn't turned on the stereo. He hadn't even picked up a magazine. He sat quietly, knees pressed together, his hands clasped loosely in his lap. If he sat very still and concentrated, Michael would come home soon. And if he didn't stop at the bank first, Johnny would tell him about his father.

...

In the crowded elevator after work, Michael smelled cigar smoke and it made him think of his Uncle Vernon. He thought of Uncle Vernon in the front room at the lake, reading dog-eared western after dog-eared western so many summers ago. "Some men," Uncle Vernon had told him once, "they think with their dicks."

...

"He's dead," Johnny said, putting the remains of his second hot dog on his plate. Mustard leaked through the torn roll into a perfectly symmetrical puddle. "He's always been dead."

A mouthful of hot dog and stale roll muffled whatever Michael might have said.

"Since before I was born." He looked at his feet. The answer wasn't there. "It's my mother." He started to cry. "She hates me. They all hate me."

Later, holding Johnny, all Michael knew for certain was what he had known all along.

"I'm trouble," Johnny murmured, undoing Michael's pants.

Michael knew that at least that was true.

"Just lie on your back," Johnny whispered.

As he lay back against the pillows, he thought he smelled cigar smoke again. But as the heat of the boy's body engulfed him, he forgot even that.

…

The screen shines blankly in front of him. No numbers. No hurtling asteroids. There is a humming in his ears and the sky opens up before him, blank as the machine's screen at first, then coming to life with the single call of a bird, cicadas in the swamp, a soft rustling of leaves and branches. He is sitting on the rusty swing in the yard and the dawn surrounds him.

After so many years he is back here again, a small boy in Roy Rogers pajamas, bare feet wet with dew. Uncle Vernon and Aunt Vivian and the others are sleeping still. He shivers slightly and yawns. He leans forward, looking up at the north attic window.

Behind the mended screen there is a flash of white, a slight movement. A gawky boy with large hands and feet is staring down at him. Borrowed red bathing trunks several sizes too large for him slide low on his hips. Dark, wet hair frames his slightly horsey face. An attempt at a moustache makes his upper lip look smudged. His wide mouth bursts open in a smile and he calls Michael's name happily, waving excitedly.

...

Johnny lay silently in the dark, listening to Michael's heavy breathing beside him. Quietly, slowly, he slid out of bed and pulled on his briefs. He turned on the kitchen light and, leaving the door ajar, returned to the bedroom. He stood looking down at Michael.

It was too bad. He liked Michael. He even liked being fucked by Michael. And that was strange because he was indifferent to being fucked. Except in dreams. There was nothing special about it. But sometimes when Michael fucked him it was exciting. He thought about it for a long time. While he was thinking about it, he got a hardon.

If things were different, he'd slide back into bed. Maybe he'd even fuck Michael's ass. He wondered what it would feel like to come in Michael's ass. But then Michael would wake up. There wasn't time for that.

He rolled his briefs down his thighs and beat off, staring down at Michael's sleeping face. When he came, he wiped his hands and belly with one of Michael's socks. He pulled his briefs back up and moved quietly to the chair where Michael's jeans had been flung. He pulled the wallet out of the hip pocket. He withdrew the plastic bank card and returned the wallet.

It was sad.

He dressed and let himself out without a sound.

…

Michael, small and excited in his Roy Rogers pajamas, rushes up the rickety back stairs. The screen door screeches and slams behind him. Bacon is crackling on the coal stove in the kitchen and Aunt Vivian is peeling potatoes at the sink.

"Someone's up real early," she smiles.

As he crosses the cracked linoleum in the parlor, Uncle Vernon looks up from *Showdown at Shotgun Ridge.* "He's waiting for you, Mikie," he says, lighting a cigar. "Upstairs."

Michael pulls open the warped wooden door and starts up the damp and crooked stairs. His legs are so short that the stairs seem frighteningly steep. He pauses halfway up.

At the top of the stairs, the boy in the red bathing trunks leans over the railing, grinning from ear to ear. Behind him, a silver-webbed mirror throws flickering sunlight in twisting patterns on the sloping ceiling.

"Look at you," the boy says. "You're littler than me."

"Gabriel," Michael whispers, his breath sending bits of dust spiraling in a patch of sunlight.

Gabriel comes down the stairs and stands just one step above him. "I've been waiting for you," he says, his voice cracking slightly. He reaches down and takes Michael's hand, leading him up the stairs. "Here," he says, picking Michael up and setting him on the edge of the big brass bed. "Let me look at you." Warm air hums, the tarpaper roof soaking up the heat of the morning sun.

Michael's legs, skinny in his Roy Rogers pajama bottoms, dangle off the edge of the bed. His little feet don't reach the floor. He starts to cry and Gabriel sits beside him, cradling him in his arms. "Shhh," Gabriel whispers. "When you were bigger, you always took care of me. Now I can take care of you." He kisses the cowlicks on the top of Michael's head. "For a little while."

Michael rubs his face against the boy's sunburned chest. Downstairs, he can hear the old Victrola being wound up. He can hear Gabriel's heart beating, strong and steady. It fills the room. And now a fox trot is playing. On the lake, an outboard motor is starting up.

The door creaks open at the foot of the stairwell. "Michael?" Aunt Vivian calls.

"Vivian," Uncle Vernon sighs from his dog-eared western in the parlor. "Leave those kids alone. Too late anyway. Their business now." The fox trot from the windup Victrola soars up the crooked stairs. Gabriel's warm lips brush Michael's forehead and the breath from them says more than words can mean.

...

Startled, Michael's eyes flew open. He was on his back in bed and Johnny was crouched over him, one hand tracing his face. Johnny's eyes were wet. "Go back to sleep," he whispered. "I was just memorizing your face."

Michael held him until he stopped crying and slept, his face burrowed into Michael's chest. Michael couldn't go back to sleep and, holding the small body against his own, he watched the grayness at the window slowly brighten, gently untangling arms and legs in time to turn off the alarm before it rang.

...

The engine of the red Mercedes makes no sound as it pulls into the carport. Elegant in his white tux, Johnny steps onto the pavement. A tall young man with a face beautiful as a blank check opens a door for him and steps back, sleek in the underwear he has cut from the glossy pages of a magazine in a dentist's office. His smile is as bright as the dentist's drill.

The steps are crooked and very steep. There are wet cistern sounds in the darkness below. Johnny descends the stairway calmly.

He hears it in the wet darkness.

Johnny, it whispers. Johnny.

He awoke on his stomach, his underwear cold and wet with come. He threw the briefs in the kitchen trash basket and took a long shower, scrubbing his body until it was beet red. He put water on to boil for his cocoa and checked the time. It was still morning. His bus wouldn't leave until 3:30.

He went to the dresser. Opening Michael's drawer, he looked down at the socks and underwear he had been washing and neatly rolling for Michael for over three months now. He put on one of Michael's old jockstraps and a pair of Michael's white wool socks, padding to the kitchen where the kettle was whistling.

The jock was loose on him, but it made him think of Michael. The socks fit all right.

He didn't want to leave. He finished the cocoa and poured himself a cold glass of milk in the Daffy Duck mug. He didn't feel like eating his Cheerios this morning. If he stayed, Michael would find out about the money.

Michael would find out about the money even if he did leave, but if he left, he and Michael wouldn't have to argue. Michael would probably hate him when he found out. It made him want to cry. But crying wouldn't solve anything.

From a desk drawer he took a snapshot of Michael. In the snapshot, Michael was dressed in a swimming suit. He was standing on the edge of a swamp. He had one tanned arm around a smaller boy with dark, wet hair and thin, knobby legs. Red bathing trunks several sizes too large for him were sliding low on his hips. Both boys were laughing as if they thought the summer afternoon would never end. It was an old snapshot, but Johnny liked it. Michael looked like Billy Idol in the snapshot. Except that he was much bigger than Billy Idol. In the snapshot, Michael looked like a god. Johnny put the snapshot in his wallet, pressed between the wad of twenty-dollar bills.

It only took him a few minutes to pack his rucksack. He left his collection of TV Guides, his records, and his poster of Billy Idol. And he left a note on the kitchen table. He left it at a right angle to the Daffy Duck mug, which he had washed and dried.

He looked back for a moment before he opened the door. His poster of Billy Idol scowled at him from the bathroom door.

"Goodbye," he mumbled.

And then he was gone.

...

On the way home from work, Michael's plastic bank card gave him a thrill. The red-orange computer lights in the window might as well have said "Go Greyhound and leave the driving to us." But that phrase wasn't in the computer's vocabulary. The lights twinkled "insufficient funds."

Michael stood on the street for a few moments. He felt cold. He didn't know which direction he was about to move in. He looked at the plastic bank card. It didn't tell him what to do.

...

Johnny looked out the bus window. It was greasy where someone had slept against it. Through the hair-oiled haze, Johnny looked at Donner Pass.

People had eaten each other there one winter. That was what had happened to the Donner Party. Johnny had read about it in a magazine. "Pass the mustard," he thought. But he didn't smile.

...

There were ten dollars in Michael's wallet. There were ninety-three cents and a Saint Christopher's medal in his right jeans pocket. Saint Christopher was the patron saint of travelers. It seemed to Michael that he had read somewhere that the Catholic Church had decanonized Saint Christopher some years back.

Michael crossed the street. At the bar he ordered a Budweiser with a whiskey chaser. There were more than ninety minutes of happy hour left. "To Saint Christopher," he said to his reflection in the mirror.

"Michael," said the face next to his in the mirror. "Remember me?"

"Sure," Michael said, turning to the boy who had come up behind him. The bottle blond in faded jeans.

"It's been awhile," the kid said. "Can I buy you another drink?"

"I don't see why not," Michael said, finishing the shot.

"If I get you drunk enough maybe you'll come home with me this time," the boy said.

"Maybe I will."

"If you come home with me," the boy said, "what will you do?"

"Fuck your brains out," Michael said.

Later, Michael had a slight headache. A dime store scarf over the shade of a battered lamp softened the dust and clutter of the cramped room, wistful and druggy, bruised as the boy, whose name was Brandy.

He had wanted to be harsh in the face of such defenselessness. Instead, he felt sad.

"It was beautiful," Brandy said. "I knew it would be beautiful." He lay with the dirty sheets pulled up to his chin, smiling stonily, one long leg sprawled over Michael's.

"I have to go," Michael said, shifting slightly. It was after midnight.

"Spend the night," Brandy whispered.

"I can't."

"I'm thirty-one years old." Brandy smiled, missing several molars. "But I've got a good body. And my ass is a work of art. Lots of guys would still pay for it."

Michael looked across the room at a framed photograph of a dead actress. She was staring into space, her face lost between expressions. There was dust on the cracked glass. It could have been an unearthed relic.

"Kiss me?" Brandy asked. As he leaned forward, a lock of unevenly bleached hair fell across his face.

...

Michael laughs and throws an arm around Johnny. With a whoop, Johnny leaps in the warm summer air, dark, wet hair flying around his laughing face. As the picture is snapped, his thin, knobby legs are suspended in a blur above uneven ground. His borrowed red bathing trunks are several sizes too large for him and they slide low on his hips.

Johnny knows the thing is down there in the trees near the water. He looks at the snapshot carefully. Just because he can't see it doesn't mean that it isn't there. He can hear it in the water. It's trying to call his name. Johnny, it's trying to say. Johnny. I'm waiting for you.

But Michael is with him. If Michael turns in his sleep, if his warm flesh grazes Johnny's beneath the comforter, the thing will go away. He can hear Michael's breathing beside him. If Michael will only move a fraction of an inch. He wants to reach out for him, but he can't move. And if he actually hears the thing call his name . . .

The loud sound that awoke him was his own groan. His legs ached and his right arm felt like ginger ale. He was on the bus and an overweight woman in a beige wool coat was staring at him. She was holding a shopping bag in her lap. Salt flats and dead trees moved by indifferently beneath the moon.

...

In the bedroom, the bed stood alone, neatly made. The rattan chair was empty and small in its corner. It was reflected in the blank screen of the television set.

On the kitchen table the note was waiting patiently beside the Daffy Duck mug. It was painstakingly neat. It had been written with a red Pentel. The word "yours" was misspelled. "Your's," it said. Like a handwritten sign in a diner: "Home Made Pie's."

Michael looked at the clock over the sink. It was almost 2 AM. He stood in the silent kitchen for a moment, holding the note. In the kitchen trash basket, a pair of boy's briefs was spying on him. "Mister," the briefs asked politely, "do you know what a fetish is?"

Michael smiled. He knew that underwear couldn't talk.

II

From the little silver frame, an amazed Kenneth Charles Cooper stares into the room from the corner of Academy Street. His left shoe is untied and his hair stands up in cowlicks. Wow, he seems to be thinking, that really looks like fun!

K.C. laughs, leaning on one elbow in the tangled sheets. "Yeah," he says. "That's me, all right."

The young man sets the framed snapshot back on the nightstand.

"You were a cute little kid." He stretches and pulls the covers up to his chin. "You look so excited."

"I always was excited," K.C. says, pulling the covers over their heads. "Still am!"

"No fair tickling!"

"Wow!" said K.C., wriggling around under the covers. "What's this?"

"Last night, I took a walk after dark," K.C.'s golden oldies tape sings. "I went down to Palisades Park, to have some fun and see what I could seeeee . . ."

AFTER DARK

Bobby was sitting on the sofa in his torn green flannel bathrobe. He was watching his favorite movie on the Late Late Show. He was lucky tonight because the reception was crystal clear.

This was his favorite scene.

Marilyn Monroe was backing away from Joseph Cotten in a bell tower. In the bell tower, the bells were playing "Night and Day."

Then the doorbell rang.

Bobby padded across the room and leaned out the window. Michael was standing on the stoop. "Hang on a second," Bobby called.

He watched Joseph Cotten strangle Marilyn Monroe as he fished in his jeans for his keys. "Yo," he called, tossing the keys out the window to Michael.

He was at the refrigerator when Michael let himself in. "We're in luck," Bobby smiled. "There's four beers left."

"Great," said Michael. He sat on the sofa and looked at the television. Jean Peters was saying something.

"The all-American dream," Bobby said, handing Michael a beer and flopping down on the sofa next to him.

"Jean Peters?" Michael asked, taking a gulp of beer.

"Freshly scrubbed and about to become one of the richest women in the world. Howard Hughes, he sure could pick 'em. Jean Harlow . . . Jane Russell . . ."

"Yeah," Michael mumbled.

"Mighty Joe Young! The friendly gorilla!"

"Mighty Joe Young?" Michael asked vaguely.

"Terry Moore!" Bobby smiled, beer glugging.

"Oh. Mighty Joe Young." Michael looked at the label on his beer can. "Since 1896," the beer can assured him. "Tum water," it said.

"Sure," Bobby laughed. "Mighty Joe Young lifts up this little stage on his back. In this night club, right?" He nudged Michael. "You must've seen that, right? On the stage is little Terry Moore. Sugar and spice and everything nice packed into a lacy little prom dress. Playing this baby grand piano . . ." Bobby's fingers flicked through the air, tickling imaginary ivories. "Beautiful dreamer . . ." he started to sing in a falsetto, "waaaa-ken to meeeeee . . . The moooooon is shiiiii-ning ju-ust for . . ."

A shudder passed through Michael's body and, with a hoarse sob, he began to cry. "Hey, slugger," Bobby said, putting his arms around him. "My voice isn't *that* bad." Bobby held him for awhile. And when it was time for him to say something, he didn't say I told you so.

He told Michael to blow his nose and take a hot shower.

"I should go home," Michael said.

"To catalogue your losses? To search out forgotten underwear?"

Michael laughed.

"Good," Bobby said. "I don't snore as much as you do and the sheets are fairly clean."

...

Johnny holds out his Daffy Duck mug. "A bit more of the bubbly," he says to Michael. Michael, with a smile, pours ginger ale into the mug.

They are sitting at the kitchen table in Michael's apartment. But the outside wall is not plaster and concrete anymore. It is old wood. The kitchen is a screened-in porch. A boy with a sunburn in red bathing trunks is walking across the uneven yard towards them. He looks familiar to Johnny.

"Michael," Johnny says. But Michael is gone. The kitchen is gone. Johnny is alone on a screened-in porch. He can hear a motorboat on the lake beyond the swamp.

The sunburned boy in the red trunks stands just outside the screen door. "What are you doing here?" the boy asks.

"I'm here with Michael," Johnny says.

"Michael isn't here," the boy says. He looks at Johnny quizzically. "You shouldn't be here," he says.

"I know who you are," Johnny says. "I have your picture in my wallet."

"Yes. We know all about you," the boy says. "Down in the swamp," he says. "It's waiting for you. It isn't supposed to be here, either."

"What is it?" Johnny feels very cold.

"It came with you," the boy says. "It must have. It isn't ours."

There is a dragging sound in the dark hallway behind Johnny.

"You'd better go," the boy says, stepping back from the screen door.

Johnny awoke with a start. The sheets were scratchy against his skin. His hair was plastered to the hard pillow. At first he couldn't think of where he was. "Oh," he said to the small, empty room. "I'm gone now."

...

Michael awakens, Bobby's sleeping body draped like a quilt across his back, one warm arm flung around his waist. He lies quietly for a moment, uncertainly, on the edge of sleep. As he yawns, rubbing his face more deeply into the pillows, he hears it:

A fox trot, scratchy and sad, is playing in the other room. He yawns again. They must have left the television on. Bobby mumbles in his sleep as Michael untangles himself from the covers and pads quietly into the living room.

"Sit with me," Gabriel says, patting the sofa beside him.

As Michael sits, the boy shifts slightly. Hitching up his red bathing trunks, he curls his body against the left side of Michael's. His sunburned flesh is warm. There is an odor of spearmint on his breath. His wiry body smells salty and sweet.

"Mikie," says Aunt Vivian from the television screen.

...

Bobby is standing on an abandoned pier. Water is lapping at its rotting pilings. He moves forward slowly, sweeping the warped planking with a flashlight, wary of missing boards. Behind him is the bedroom, blinds drawn against the fog that whispers around him now, so far from shore.

He is wearing the letter sweater that Michael gave him the first summer they lived together in Baltimore, the city of dead sailors, the sweater that he lost from a coat rack in a crowded bar ten years ago. There is a hole from a cigarette burn in the right pocket. The hole was mended with darning thread by Michael's Aunt Vivian three years before Bobby met Michael.

The pale beam of the flashlight sweeps ahead of him. He shivers. Michael is out there somewhere, far beyond him. And there's something else. Something moving in the water beneath him, from slippery piling to slippery piling.

...

"It's like television," Aunt Vivian says from the screen of Bobby's television.

"You can see us and hear us. But we're somewhere else, too."

"More like Burns and Allen than those cop shows, though," says Uncle Vernon, lighting a cigar.

"We're what you want to remember. You, you're what we want to remember, too. Little dots and static. Like a broadcast."

"But you can feel us," says Gabriel, his head on Michael's shoulder. "And we can feel you. We can feel you, too."

"Can't say how," Uncle Vernon says, shaking his head and picking up his dog-eared copy of *The Ghostriders of the Purple Sage*. "No words in any language can do it. Infinity. Eternity. What the hell are they? Words, that's all. Fence somebody tried to put around reality. Reality. There's another one." Uncle Vernon snorts. "You think if they could trap a moonbeam in a bottle they wouldn't do it?"

"See," Aunt Vivian smiles, "it doesn't stop."

"Think of all the possibilities." Uncle Vernon shakes his head. "All the bullshit that's been said and written and put in rulebooks. All you'll ever get for yourself is the biggest headache you wish you never had."

"You got to be careful, Mikie." Aunt Vivian frowns. "Call the dead and it ain't always who you love that comes."

"Something else is getting in," Gabriel says softly. "Something bad."

"Bad." Uncle Vernon shakes his head. "Words again. Think add and subtract. Give or take away."

"Eternity," Gabriel whispers. "And nothing."

...

Bobby shivered and clawed at the pillow, waking. He had kicked the covers off his side of the bed. Michael's side was empty. But Michael's clothes were still draped over the back of the wicker chair. He heard the television in the other room. With a yawn, he got up and pulled on his robe.

In the living room, Michael was asleep on the couch facing a fat man on the television set. The fat man was surrounded by furniture. "Se habla credit," the fat man said.

Bobby got a blanket from the bedroom and covered Michael. On the television, Lex Barker was rescuing a kid in red bathing trunks from an alligator in a Technicolor swamp.

"Sleep tight, sport," Bobby whispered, turning off the television.

When the kettle began to whistle, Bobby realized that all the coffee cups were dirty.

"You are a disaster area," he said to the kitchen. The kitchen did not reply. He rinsed out yesterday's coffee cup. He had rinsed out the same cup almost every morning for the past twelve years.

He smiled at the cup. Although there was a chip on the lip, the transfer was still on it. Michael had ordered two of them from a photo store in Baltimore twelve years ago.

Two tall young men laughed at him from the photo transfer. The blond had his right arm draped around the shoulders of the slighter brunet, who was wearing a white and gold letter sweater. The old pier stretched on endlessly behind them and the Baltimore sun rode far above the tide.

Michael's Aunt Vivian had taken the picture one Memorial Day weekend with her battered Brownie Starflash.

Michael had lost his cup years ago.

...

Johnny was looking through record bins. He had bought a down jacket at a Goodwill a few hours earlier and he was wearing it now. It was cold in this city.

He looked at a Billy Idol album. Billy Idol snarled at him, coiled tightly in red plastic pants. Johnny wanted the album, but he knew it would be a waste of money. He didn't have a stereo at the Y.

The down jacket had only one tear in it. After buying it, he had a little over $100 left. As soon as he made some money, he'd get a better jacket. And he'd get a stereo. And he wouldn't be staying at the Y anymore.

He'd buy all the Billy Idol records he wanted.

He thumbed idly through the bin.

He flipped past it, before he realized what he'd seen. He flipped back to it. It was a group he's never heard of.

Imago.

The vibrant colors of the photograph had been processed on grooved layers of plastic, giving it not only the illusion of depth, but that of movement.

The sunburned chest of the boy in red bathing trunks rose and fell as he leaped into the summer air again and again, his mouth opening and closing in a silent whoop of delight. His hair whipped wet and dark around his joyous face, catching the sunlight.

Johnny felt a numbing chill, catching the heavy, sweet scent of lilacs.

In the deepest layers of plastic, in the background of the photograph, within the tangled trees and undergrowth of the swamp, something moved furtively, its movements corresponding to the opening and closing of the leaping boy's mouth.

With cold hands, Johnny shoved the record back into the bin. He stumbled backwards.

Leaving the store, he thought he heard something. He thought he heard his name being called quietly.

Johnny, the voice said. Johnny. Come here . . .

. . .

At the top of the crooked stairs, Michael turns on his side. The old brass bed creaks beneath him. Warm air drifts down from the weather-stained ceiling, soaking in from the tarpaper roof. Through the torn green shades the morning sun falls in dusty streamers across the warped wooden floorboards. Gabriel sighs and leans back against the pillows, a thin sheen of sweat on his sunburned chest.

"What if I never wake up?" Michael says softly.

"You will wither and die," says Gabriel.

On the other side of the musty stairwell, a speck of light on the silver-webbed mirror explodes, shooting shards of light into the space between the faded flowers on the wall. And the walls, with their secrets, turn to smoke, whispering softly through the clear, blank sky that dreams above.

Michael opened damp eyes, tangled in Bobby's blanket. The dead screen of the television stared at him blindly. From the kitchen, he heard Bobby singing along with the radio. Bobby and breakfast with the radio. Michael smiled, remembering breakfasts in Baltimore.

"Last night I took a walk after dark," sang Bobby and the radio, "I went down to Palisades Park . . ."

...

Johnny sat on the edge of his bed at the Y. He was paid up through the week. He flipped through his new TV Guide. He read the capsule reviews of each movie that was showing on television in that city this afternoon. There were some good ones. There was an awful one, too. One that he had seen when he was just a little kid. He'd watched it with two of his older brothers and his oldest sister.

It was before Mommy married her second husband. It was late at night and Mommy was working at the phone company. Lots of times, his brothers and sisters would let him stay up late with them. Mommy didn't like them to stay up late on school nights. But when Mommy was at the phone company there wasn't much she could do about it.

He was really very little when they watched that awful movie on the old Zenith. When Mommy married her second husband they got a new television. And his older brothers and sisters didn't stay around the house much after Mommy's second husband moved in. It had been just him and Tommy, then. He and Tommy had been the only little ones.

He remembered that he had his little blanket with the rabbits on it. And his flannel pajamas had feet in them. His oldest sister had held him on her lap and, when the titles had come on, she had read them aloud to him. He couldn't read yet then. Tommy couldn't read yet, either. But Tommy was already asleep that night when they watched the awful movie.

The music on the television was scary. It was loud and soft at the same time. And it made you shiver and think that maybe you had to go to the bathroom. Except you wouldn't want to go because the bathroom was outside and it was real dark out there.

The people were all dressed funny and that made it kind of creepy, too. "It's a very old movie," his older sister had told them. Sometimes when you think about things a long time ago, so long ago that it was before you were born, it's really scary. Because, if you're not careful, you could start to wonder what it's like not to be. To be nothing at all. And sometimes that could give you nightmares, thinking about being nothing at all.

In the swamp, this dead man was wandering around. And you couldn't see him too good, because of the fog and it was night in the swamp. They said he'd been hanged right there in the swamp. And he walked around at night, all stiff and his arms hung loose and funny. And his head was bent off to the side of his neck on account of his being hanged by a rope until he was dead.

And for a long time after that, you'd dream about the Strangler. And sometimes you'd get the Strangler mixed up in your head with Mommy's second husband. On the nights when the bad things happened.

Johnny closed the TV Guide. There wasn't a television in his room at the Y. They had one in the lounge downstairs. But he didn't like to go in there. Because the men in there would look at him funny. And he knew what they wanted. He knew that, all right. But if they had what he needed, they wouldn't be staying in a little room at the YMCA.

But he wouldn't watch that movie about the Strangler anyway. If he had a television in his room, he'd watch Robert Wagner and Joanne Woodward in *A Kiss Before Dying*. That was on at three this afternoon. But he wouldn't sit in the lounge downstairs. Not even if they had MTV and Billy Idol was on.

…

Bobby had walked the half block up the hill to Michael's building with him. He would have liked to go in with him, but he'd done all he could do. He'd lent him $400 so he could make his rent. He'd offered to buy him dinner. He'd have liked to have offered him more. He wished Michael hadn't wanted to be alone. Bobby didn't want to be alone.

Bobby wanted to be twenty-one years old again. He wanted to walk into the Drunken Sailor in Baltimore and see a blond giant at the end of the bar. He wanted the blond god to look up at him and smile. He wanted to drift through the crowd towards him. He wanted to feel the touch of his hand for the first time again. He wanted to hear: My name is Michael. What's yours?

But Baltimore was several thousand miles and over a decade away.

So Bobby found himself walking into The Lost Cause. Saturday night, he thought. Might as well have a drink.

…

Johnny walked past a large supermarket as its red and blue sign blinked off for the night. He followed the pavement. He looked for the lights.

He waited for a traffic light, scanning cars for their secrets. The street to his left looked right. Neon. Darkness. More neon. Men in pairs, in packs, and drifting—so casually—alone.

Crossing the street, he stepped onto the stained curb, walking taller than his sixty-two inches, his pale face solemn, a carefully assembled mask of confused adolescence. Here, piggy, he said to himself, piggy, piggy, piggy . . . He smiled.

"Johnny," someone whispered from a darkened doorway.

He stopped and turned towards the shadows.

"It's dangerous, Johnny," said the sunburned boy in red bathing trunks. As he stepped into the glare of the streetlights, he faded into gray mist. It only lasted an instant. Johnny stared at the empty air before him.

. . .

Bobby was playing Video Stud. He had spent over ten dollars and hadn't even gotten the Fireman down to his underpants. The Fireman grinned at him in freeze frame, his hand frozen halfway up the thick rubber shaft of his hose.

"You're Michael's friend, aren't you?" said a husky voice at his shoulder.

"Yes," Bobby said, lighting a cigarette and turning to face the kid in the ragged jeans.

"Your name is Bobby, isn't it?"

"Right again," Bobby said.

"That's what I thought." He glanced stonily at the video screen. "That's a big hose, isn't it?"

Bobby cleared his throat.

"My name is Brandy," the kid said. "Michael fucked me last night." He smiled. "Will you fuck me tonight?"

...

At 11:00 that evening, one of Michael's neighbors came in from the movies. He went to the kitchen to make some tea. Waiting for the water to boil, he glanced out the window. In a window across the courtyard, he saw a naked blond man sitting in a rattan chair with a can of beer in his hand. The only light in the darkened room came from a television set.

He didn't know the man. But he looked at him until the kettle boiled. He wasn't hard to look at.

On the television screen, Suzy Parker was weeping on a fire escape. She was going through Louis Jourdan's garbage can, desperately searching for souvenirs among the clumps of spoiled food and spent cans.

Michael thought of the soiled underpants in the kitchen trash basket.

...

Johnny shivered, leaning against a phone booth in front of an all-night doughnut shop. He was tired. That's all it was.

He lit a cigarette and scanned the street. A Lincoln Continental crawled past and slowed to a stop several feet from him. The passenger door swung open. As he slid onto the leather seat, the old man said, "You're not like the others. I've been watching you."

Johnny stared at the old man, his face going ashen.

"You shouldn't smoke, you know," the old man said. "It's not good for you." He laughed. "Shut the door, Johnny," he said. "Let me take you for a ride."

The old man's face seemed to be melting.

With a scream, Johnny leaped to the street and hurtled down the sidewalk, colliding with a young man in jeans and a bomber jacket.

"Hey," the young man said.

Johnny began to cry.

"Hey," the young man repeated, more softly this time. "What's the matter?"

Leaning against the young man, Johnny looked over his shoulder. The Lincoln Continental was gone. "Pig," he said under his breath. "A man," Johnny said to the young man. "He . . ." Johnny wasn't sure whether he was crying for himself or for the benefit of the young man.

"Do you want to come with me?" the young man asked.

Johnny nodded.

"My name's Kenneth Charles Cooper," the young man grinned. "But if you smile, I'll let you call me K.C."

. . .

Hazy from the boy's hashish, Bobby was overpowered by the bed, betrayed by his underpants and socks. Motionless, he leaned slightly in the overheated room.

Naked, Brandy turned to face him, the dim, blue light behind   masking his features. As the boy moved slowly towards him, the air rippled between them, water in a tropical aquarium, angelfish and sea horses turning slowly, tank bubbles rising, white pebbles, clear glass marbles, the Land of the Lost, where children's toys and dreams are sometimes found.

The boy's wiry arms went around him and their bodies pressed t   her. With a shock, Bobby realized the body stretched against him was   al to his own. If the flesh hadn't been warm, he could have been alone   g himself flat against a full-length mirror.

Gently, Brandy ran the tip of his right forefinger   pale crescent scar below Bobby's navel. "I've had appendicitis,   he whispered. "Sit down," he smiled, slipping Bobby's underpants dov   He lifted each leg in turn and removed the socks.

One black.

One blue.

"We almost match," he said, stretching out on the bed. With a sigh he turned over onto his stomach, burying his head in the pillows. "Now fuck me," he whispered. "Fuck me like Michael would fuck you."

. . .

Johnny leaned back on the couch and smiled. The young man was over six-feet tall with a rangy walk and legs that were bowed enough to set off the high curve of his buttocks. Large, long fingered hands, feet that looked like a jack rabbit's in size thirteen white sneakers, a cute face framed by a mass of dark cowlicks. If Johnny had dreamed him, he couldn't have been better.

The apartment wasn't cheap, either, so he probably had money, too. This wasn't turning out to be such a bad night, after all. If he played his hand right, it might be more. This guy wasn't as old as Michael, so he'd have to work a little harder. He unbuttoned the top three buttons of his plaid shirt, his pulse quickening at the equally pleasant prospects of his two favorite things:

Warm semen and cold cash.

"I'm going to turn in now," K.C. yawned. "Just make yourself at home. Hop up," he said, tossing fresh sheets and a blanket onto a leather hassock, "and I'll help you make up the couch."

Johnny's face fell. He sighed and looked at his feet.

"Are you okay?" K.C. asked.

Johnny nodded, frowning slightly. "K.C.?"

"Yeah?"

"Why do you want me to sleep on the couch?" Johnny whispered, crooking his forefinger in the fly of K.C.'s jeans.

K.C. laughed.

"Don't you like me?" Johnny asked. He cocked his head and looked up at K.C. Slipping his hand inside K.C.'s briefs, he pouted, making automobile sounds, manipulating K.C.'s sex as if it were a stick shift.

It hung on a wall behind them, the framed page from a children's book. From beneath the plexiglass, a toy soldier peered down at them, sad face lost in shadows.

. . .

Rusty weather stains swirled on the ancient wallpaper, transforming faded fleur-de-lys into phantom ships and storm-tossed sailors. Brandy's body was warm and moist against his own. Legs tangled in the torn top sheet. The radiator hissed, a faceless metal sphinx crouching in a bone-strewn corner.

Smiling, Brandy stretched against him, one long arm reaching over him to flip the switch on a battered transistor radio. With a sigh, he settled back against Bobby's side, his scruffy head burrowing into the hollow of his shoulder.

"You'll never know how great a kiss can feel," the transistor sang, "When you stop at the top of a Ferris wheel . . . When I fell in love, down at Palisades Park . . ."

"Last night," Brandy whispered, bringing one scabby knuckled hand to Bobby's cheek, "I dreamed I was you." He brushed his lips against Bobby's throat.

Bobby was staring at a postcard thumbtacked to the wall by the bed: from a stretch of land deserted by night, an endless pier leaned into the stormy tide, mossy pilings drowning in spray. Baltimore, Bobby thought. Baltimore.

"I was way off in the dark somewhere on the water . . . It was dark and the water was real deep? And at first I was scared because I was all alone. But then I knew I wasn't. Because I was you."

No. It wasn't Baltimore. It only looked like Baltimore because he was stoned. And he wasn't lying against himself. He wasn't lying against himself, either.

. . .

Michael's neighbor awoke from a vague dream. Yawning, he glanced at the clock. It was 4:38 AM. He went to the bathroom and relieved himself. His mouth was fetid with the taste of too many cigarettes the night before. On his way to the refrigerator, he noticed an odd light across the courtyard. In the window where he had seen the naked blond over five hours ago, there was a figure bathed in a nimbus of light formed by the television behind it.

Slowly, the figure turned its back to the window and sat in a chair. It was a sunburned boy in red bathing trunks.

Across the courtyard, Michael opened his eyes, a dream of Baltimore sinking into the rumpled pillows he was embracing. The television was on.

"I don't know," Della Street was saying to Perry Mason. "It's about this Johnny Cortez case."

"Michael," Gabriel whispered from the rattan chair. "Are you awake?" He leaned forward, turning the sound down on the television set. "I have to tell you something," he said softly. Perry Mason, more eloquent in silence, began to address the jury.

...

Johnny is sitting in the Colonial Movie Theatre. On the screen, his brother Tommy is stumbling through a mist-shrouded swamp. Music crackles loud and soft at once through the ancient speakers. It falters and fades, replaced by the growl of static. Beneath Johnny's feet, the floor is sticky from spilled Dr. Pepper. In close-up, Tommy's four-year-old face stares at him in freeze frame, eyes wide in terror.

"Please remain seated," the manager's voice wheezes over the speakers. "It is ten o'clock—I repeat, please remain seated—it is time for the Ceremony of Old Men."

In the darkness beside him, there is a soft sigh. The lights are coming up slightly, fading the mammoth shadow of his brother's face on the torn screen. There are sounds of furtive movement in the musty half-light. There is the odor of dust and rotting velvet. That and something else—stale, sharp, and vaguely feral.

All around him, old men, raincoats wrinkled, are slowly coming to their feet, old bones creaking, wine breath coming in short gasps.

On the screen, Tommy screams.

"Johnny," the voice whispers in his ear. "Johnny . . ." In the strangled half-light around him, the rustling increases and there is sudden laughter, ripe and brutal, the barking of hyenas.

As Tommy's screams faded, Johnny's eyes flew open. Cold with sweat, he was lying in bed in the back bedroom. The bed that *they* slept in. Mommy and her second husband. He was naked. In a pool of moonlight, he saw his torn underwear on the uneven floorboards. Then he heard it. The breathing. Deep, even, droning. And Johnny could smell the whiskey, sweet as vomit in the cramped and stuffy room. On the other side of the straw-mattressed bed, the broad back was tangled in the homespun covers.

Johnny's body ached and he realized, dully, that between his legs he was bleeding. He wanted to scream for Mommy. But he knew she wasn't here. Mommy was gone. Or he wouldn't be here. In this room. With him.

Holding his breath, he climbed out of bed. A floorboard creaked beneath his feet and he froze, motionless as a rabbit on a highway. A half-formed word rose from the old brass bed. A groan. And then, the even, drunken breathing.

Johnny pulled on the torn underpants. The warped door was ajar. Johnny crept towards it, shivering.

...

The little wooden and steel gondola rattles and swings in the neon air as the creaking machinery grinds to a stop. Bobby's knuckles are white on the iron bar across their laps.

"Kiss me," Michael says.

Beneath them, the park stretches its tawdry arms through the Baltimore night. Tinny music, rancid grease, screams, and laughter swim through the filthy air. When Bobby was a little kid, he used to think he could smell polio in the air here. And his legs would start to ache from it, the taffy apple disease. Every time he touched something, his mother would dab at his hands with a handkerchief soaked in alcohol.

The wheel grinds forward, dipping them into the night. The canvas broadsides rush upwards: Eeeka the Wild Girl, eating a sailor's arm; Hitler's Blonde Love Slave, blindfolded before a firing squad of roustabouts; and the Boy in Red Bathing Trunks, waving wildly, skinny arms flailing.

A Calliope fox trot soars as the merry-go-round careens up to meet them. Perched on tiny horses and elephants, pale riders wave. Beyond the ropes of brightly colored lights, the bay pounds against the old pier.

...

His stomach in a knot, Johnny stumbled through the doorway. His bare feet were on cool tile. This wasn't the hallway. He groped in the dark for the light switch.

Light flooded the small room. It was a bathroom. Black and white tile. Red tub, toilet, and lavabowl. Chrome fixtures. Mirrors with tube lighting . . . Disoriented, he stared at himself in one of the full-length mirrors. In Mommy's house, the toilet was outside on the back lawn.

He stared at himself in the mirrors. He was bigger. There was dark hair in his armpits, below his navel. He must be dreaming . . .

In the dark room he has just left, he heard the bedsprings creak. "Johnny?" the voice called from the darkness. Johnny backed against the sink, his heart racing. He started to cry.

"Johnny?" the voice called again. His voice. He was coming for him. He was going to hurt him again.

Johnny held his breath as the man stepped through the door. His body seemed to blot out the doorframe, filling the room. He smelled of whiskey and sweat and harm. His flesh was multiplied in the mirrors, each reflection colliding with another until he became a hulking, naked legion. Flattened against the wall, Johnny opened and closed his mouth soundlessly . . . His hand scrabbled along the black porcelain counter.

"Are you okay?" the man said. He stepped forward. As he touched Johnny's arm, Johnny's hand closed on a straight razor.

There was only one scream and it ended abruptly in a bubbling sound that made Johnny want to vomit. But he held his ground. He pressed his advantage.

And the mirrors and tile were running red. Redness pumped everywhere. It was hot against his face, running down his body, soaking his underpants.

But this time, it wasn't his blood. No. Not his.

…

"You won't let me go," Gabriel whispers, his sunburned flesh huddled against Michael. "But if you don't, you can't go on."

The walls are shifting, shimmering.

"We were new," Gabriel says. "We were new then."

Michael's flesh tingles, warm, cold, warm, shifting with the walls, the night. There's an odor of damp, a creaking of boards, the buzzing of cicadas. Blackness washes through the room. Michael watches breathlessly as a summer night blossoms around him. Uneven ground, wild berry bushes, the swamp, moonlight and distant music wavering on the water, the funereal sweetness of lilacs. The camp looms to their left, its roof tumbled in, walls leaning oddly, the rear stairway no more than a jumble of rotting boards.

"This isn't how you remember it, is it, Michael?" Gabriel whispers.

He backs away from Michael, wading through marsh grass, bare feet splashing in the brackish shallows of the swamp. "New," Gabriel calls from a stand of willows.

Behind him, Michael hears a groaning of old wood. A patch of golden light leaps across the lawn, throwing his now lanky shadow halfway to the shallows.

As he turns towards the light, he sees something move furtively in the swamp, just beyond his line of vision. The cicadas are silent now.

"Michael," Aunt Vivian calls from the upstairs window. "Come in here, honey. Come in and let him go."

...

Johnny, cold hands braced on the toilet bowl, knees on cold tile. His head ached. Behind him, surrounding him in the ghastly high-tech mirrors, the torn bag of flesh that had once been a young man nicknamed K.C. sprawled in its seeping fluids.

Still gagging, Johnny stepped over it and into the tub, pulling the black plastic curtain closed behind him. Hot water cascaded over his body.

He toweled off in the bedroom. After taking clean underpants from a pine scented drawer, he dressed quickly. He checked the pockets of K.C.'s jeans. He slid the alligator wallet into his jacket pocket automatically, without even checking its contents. He shut the door behind him gently, as if not to wake K.C. He felt a little better after descending the service stairs to the street.

At the Y, he folded his clothing carefully into his rucksack.

...

The crowds are far behind Bobby now. In tan chinos and Michael's letter sweater, he is standing in the wind that is pounding off the bay. In the distance, the park's mechanical roar and sadly tinny music are hushed in the summer wind, packed away like a child's first baby tooth, nested in cotton in a tiny box at the back of some forgotten drawer with foil-wrapped bits of decaying wedding cake, snippets of the hair of children long dead, the silt of face powder, three rhinestones from a lost earring.

As he steps onto the worn boards of the old pier, he hears his name on the wind.

"Hold up, Bobby." Michael's Uncle Vernon calls. "See you're in this, too," he smiles, stepping onto the pier.

"In what?" asks Bobby, the wind ruffling his hair.

"Good question," Vernon rumbles, managing to light a cigar in the wind. "How long's it been, kid?"

...

Aunt Vivian touches Michael's shoulder lightly at the top of the crooked stairs. The attic smells musty. A trapped fly is buzzing in a darkened corner. "You were up here that night, weren't you?"

"Let's go downstairs," Michael whispers.

She shakes her head. "Look out there. Again."

The music from the old hotel drifts across the shallows again, just as it did that night so long ago. A waltz in three-quarter time, faint as the face on the silver moon. At the end of the old wooden walkway, the slight figure in red bathing trunks turns and waves, stepping into the rowboat.

"This is where it ended, Mikie," Aunt Vivian whispers.

Leaning against the window frame, Michael sees Gabriel's ball-point signature on the heavy plaster cast on his right leg. The word "yours" is misspelled. "Your's until Niagara Falls, Gabriel," it says. His seersucker pajama leg is slit up the side to accommodate the cast's bulk.

"I should have gone with him."

"Your leg was broken," Aunt Vivian smiles.

"I meant just now. I should have followed him into the swamp."

"Until tonight you could have, Mikie. For awhile, at least."

Michael slaps a mosquito that has settled on his chest. A smear of blood blooms on the white seersucker.

"There's something else out there, Mikie. It isn't ours."

Beyond the stand of willows, Michael can see something moving furtively. A shadowy form shambles stiffly through the marsh grass and poison sumac, arms hanging loosely, lost in the thick fog that is pouring off the lake like Dry Ice. It moves spasmodically, a badly strung marionette, ungainly legs in torn coveralls, scuttling crablike through the mud and undergrowth, its head at an impossible angle.

The music drifting from the old hotel is changing now. It falters and fades, cracking loud and soft at once. A small boy in torn pajamas stumbles through the shallows, his terrified, mud-spattered face pale as the smoky fog. "Johnny!" the child screams. "Johnny!"

· · ·

"You're still close to Mikie," Vernon says, skipping a sand dollar on the waves of the bay. "This far." He pauses, squinting into the wind. "How far you want to go?"

Bobby jams his fists into the pockets of his chinos. He looks into Vernon's whisker-stubbled smile and shivers.

"Yep," Vernon nods. "That's what I mean. Can you hack it, kid?"

The wind is stronger now. It whines around them, insistent and mournful. And then Bobby hears something else. Something moving in the water beneath them, splashing from slippery piling to slippery piling.

· · ·

Sunlight was seeping through the torn paper shades and the room was oppressively warm. Bobby stared at the stained plaster of the low ceiling. Brandy was asleep against him, breathing loudly through his mouth, like a child with a head cold, his open lips wet against Bobby's chest. With a deep sigh, the boy squirmed closer, his stiff sex poking Bobby's leg blindly.

Brains, Bobby thought. Brains and hearts. They're organs, too. The boy moaned against him. But they don't heat up as quickly.

…

Cramped and groggy, Michael opened his eyes. Bright sunlight flooded the room. He was sitting in the rattan chair facing the television set.

"The scientific term is actually 'metempsychosis'," an intense man with a beard and glasses was telling a woman dressed in a Frederick's of Hollywood version of a vampire's gown. "The transmogrification of souls, or of the 'anima' as the Jungians would call it. The word 'reincarnation' has come to have so many cryptoreligious connotations that it no longer serves the scientific purpose."

"We've been talking to Dr. Curtis Renfield," the young woman deadpanned, flashing a hardcover book in a metallic silver jacket, "author of *Beyond the Pale: Paranormal for the Eighties*. And now," she smiled, flashing celluloid fangs, "back to our movie, *Souls in Limbo*."

Michael leaned forward and turned off the set. His head pounded dully.

…

Laughing, Brandy hopped out of bed and flipped on the television set, an old Korean portable with torn tin foil on its bent rabbit ears. "Coffee," he promised, clanking through the dirty dishes in the chipped enamel sink. "It's instant," he said, putting a dented saucepan on the hot plate, "but it's caffeine."

"Wonderful," Bobby smiled from the wreckage of the bed.

"Nothing can stop him," the old man on the television said. "You cannot kill the dead."

A blond woman turned slowly in the shadows, squaring padded shoulders. "There must be a way." Her lower lip trembled as the music rose behind her.

"Hey," said Brandy, crawling back into bed. "This movie's great, man! I saw it when I was a little kid."

"He will walk the night until someone comes to him willingly, out of love," the old man said. "Someone willing to die for the love of another."

"It's a classic," Brandy said. "Like this."

"Give me a break," Bobby laughed, shoving Brandy's hand away.

Thick clouds of Dry Ice swept across the television screen. There, in a stand of willows smothered in Spanish moss, a gaunt figure loomed, faceless in the dim studio twilight. Slowly, the camera tracked through the chemical fog, turning, turning. A light was burning in the window of a weathered building at the edge of the swamp. The camera swept closer now, peering into a rustic kitchen. An old woman in jeans, a flannel shirt, and an apron stood by the sink, souvenir sombreros hanging on the wall behind her. She was holding a frying pan. She turned to an old man sitting at the kitchen table reading a dog-eared pulp western.

"Dark now," she said. "And he's still got the boat out."

The old man looked up from his book. "Nothing we can do," he said. "Now." He shook his head and lit a cigar.

III

Imagine a late Friday afternoon in October in a less complicated time. Jack Kennedy is in the White House. Marilyn Monroe is on the screen. And Kenneth Charles Cooper has just run all the way up Academy Street, making sure that his Speed King sneakers don't hit any of the cracks in the leaf-strewn sidewalk.

In his room, he dumps his schoolbooks on the floor ("K.C.," his mom is always telling him, "I don't for the life of me see why you have to drop things on the floor. You're twelve years old. That's old enough to yaaada yaada yaada . . .") He switches on the radio and flops on the bed, eagerly opening the newest issue of Weird Galaxies.

Weird Galaxies *is the best magazine in the world.*

And Time Warp of the Evil Dead *is the best serial* Weird Galaxies *has ever printed.*

Popping three pieces of Fleer's Double Bubble in his mouth, tabling the free wax paper comics for later, K.C. turns eagerly to page 45:

Shivering, Eve awoke, pulling the torn remnants of the nearly translucent gown around her. In the pale light of dawn, she noted their surroundings with dismay. They were no longer in the decompression chamber, but in the bedroom of some rustic cabin. She gasped, her heart beating faster beneath her full breasts which were barely covered by the insufficient material. She had fallen asleep on her watch. "Captain Masters," she cried. "Captain Masters—wake up!"

Masters leapt to his feet beside her, sharp mind and sinewy body instantly alert. "Eve," he said briskly, putting one muscular arm around her protectively, pulling her nearly naked body against his treelike chest. She shuddered as she felt his flesh against hers. "What is it?" he cried.

"I . . ." Her cheeks were hot with embarrassment, not only from her failure to keep watch, but from their relative state of undress. "I fell asleep!"

"Good Lord!" Masters intoned.

"Where are we?" Eve whispered, her body tingling against her protector's.

"I have no idea," Masters ejaculated. "Unless . . ."

"What?" Eve breathed, small against his chest.

"Out the window there," Masters said tersely.

"May God protect us," Eve shuddered.

"Yes," said Masters, squaring his massive shoulders. "Jackal Swamp."

"No," Eve sobbed. "Not the Dream Corral, where one who enters may never again return! A maze of remembered places..."

"And each egress blocked," Masters interjected with a sober nod. "Blank electromagnetic walls on three sides..."

"And, "Eve exclaimed piteously, "the hideous Guardians of Jackal Swamp holding sway on the fourth!"

"It is not a pretty picture," Masters ruminated.

Wow, K.C. thinks. The Dream Corral! The hunting preserve of the Evil Dead! In The Space Mushrooms of the Evil Dead, *Captain Masters and the haunted Blanche Winters had found a crazed wanderer who had escaped from the Dream Corral, his mind completely destroyed by the Guardians and his tongue cut out by the Evil Dead themselves.*

Everybody who woke up in the Dream Corral thought they were safe in some happy place from their past. Of course, Captain Masters and Eve knew better. Before dying in a skirmish with the dreaded Demons of Inertia, Blanche Winters had projected herself astrally into the Corral of Dreams. She had died in Captain Masters' arms. But not before divulging the secret of the Dream Corral:

The Dream Corral was just an illusion. There were all these rooms and they interconnected, so in one room you would think you were in New York. But if you walked through the door you would be in another room that looked like it was in your hometown, or even like it was on the planet Akron. But it was just like a movie set, because it wasn't any of these places!

It was a trap devised by the Evil Dead so they could feed on you.

Boy, those Evil Dead. Were they ever mean!

Then again, the Evil Dead weren't really dead at all. Captain Masters had explained that to Eve right after he had rescued her from the nefarious Commander Ennui in The Cosmic Snares of the Evil Dead:

> "A devilish trick," Masters exclaimed, thoughtfully covering Eve's shivering nakedness with the remnants of his torn tunic. "The Evil Dead are not the Dead at all!"
>
> "Then that was not really my poor murdered brother Zoltan?" Eve gasped, her lovely breasts heaving beneath the flimsy material of Masters' shredded garment.
>
> "The Forces of Chaos," Masters said forcefully. "They take the shape of the Dead since they have no shape of their own!"

K.C. turned back to the picture of Captain Masters and Eve on page 45.

Boy, Weird Galaxies *had some of the best artists in the world working for them. It was almost as if you could reach out and touch the flesh. And the ink smelled good, too. A little like airplane glue.*

"And I'll never," the radio sang. *"No, I'll never . . . dance again . . . No, I'll never . . . never . . . never . . ."*

SNAPSHOTS

Behind the broken glass of her dime store frame, the dead actress surveyed the devastated room. Brandy was asleep. Brandy was alone.

"I don't live far," Michael says to him in the smoky gloom. The jukebox is blaring: "Last night I took a walk after dark . . ." As they step into the summer night, Brandy realizes that they are in Baltimore. He has never been in Baltimore, but the cramped streets seem familiar, as if this were a dream.

Halfway down a block of row houses, just beyond a burned out streetlamp, Michael leans down and kisses him. "You know," he smiles, "you haven't told me your name."

"Bobby," Brandy smiles up to him.

"Come on in, Bobby," says Michael.

At the top of the steps Brandy turns for a moment. Someone is standing in the street at the end of the block, watching them. A young man just over five feet tall with a shock of black hair. If Brandy were closer, he would see that the young man's left eye doesn't track right. And if the light were better, he would see that the young man is not alone . . .

. . .

There is a faint odor of carbon monoxide in the old bullet-shaped Nash as its tires hum over the blacktop, eagerly riding out the distance. The wool seat itches against Michael's bare back. On the radio, a fox trot is playing on a station that went off the air decades ago.

Aunt Vivian pulls the old Nash over to the shoulder of the road. The night is clear and there is a clean wind. "The path is over there, Mikie," she says softly.

Michael gets out of the car. Just beyond a weed-tangled drainage ditch, the path to the bay begins its descent.

"We'll see you another night, Mikie," Aunt Vivian smiles. "But don't come alone. Bring Bobby with you." She seems smaller in the big old car. She waves and, as Michael pauses on the steep path, she pulls the car into gear and turns back onto the highway. She beeps the horn twice as the taillights disappear around a wooded bend.

The moonlight falls in patterns on the rocky shore beneath the pier and, several feet beyond him, the water laps insistently against the weathered pilings. "I've missed you," Bobby whispers, moving from the deeper shadows. "It seems like years."

"I was with you someplace," Michael murmurs. "But I don't know where. A terrible little room. The sheets were filthy."

...

"No," Bobby moaned into his pillow. "That wasn't me."

He turned over with a gasp. Sunlight streamed in the window. The covers were tangled and half off the bed. He felt breathless and sweaty, but he lay quietly, careful not to disturb Michael, whose sleeping body sprawled against his own.

He looked at the dreaming face he'd first seen in Baltimore over twelve years ago, turned toward him now on the rumpled sheets, chin tucked slightly behind one round, broad shoulder.

The fine spider's web of lines around the eyes, deeper folds along the full lips, a human erosion that is the signature of passion, flesh growing more eager with each passing year to reveal what is inside it, muscle, sinew, and the final secret of blankly staring bone.

He smiled and shifted slightly, easing his body more fully against the strand of warm sleeping flesh.

It was like a dream, being lost in Michael again.

. . .

It was a large city, but flat, dirty, and uninteresting. Johnny felt trapped, as if he had been swallowed by the country itself, a bland and shapeless creature in a double-knit suit.

In the ugly room, he opened the alligator wallet. He counted the money carefully for the sixth time today. Less than ninety dollars in bills and change. There had been a lot of money in the wallet. But that had been two weeks and five hundred miles ago.

He had thrown out the identification. But he had left some of the snapshots in the little plastic windows. He looked at them again. Most of the pictures were from photobooths. Some had phone numbers scrawled on the back. If things were different, he might have called some of the numbers. All of the young men were attractive. They all smiled at him. He wondered what it would be like to sleep with them. There was a slightly faded Polaroid of K.C., too. He was laughing in surprise, a blurred towel in his right hand barely obscuring his genitals. A friend of his must have taken it as a goof.

Johnny knew that K.C. had enjoyed fucking him. Maybe he would have asked Johnny to move in with him. It had been a nice apartment. And he might have met all these other young men, too. He sighed and flipped past the plastic sealed K.C. The next window had held K.C.'s driver's license. Johnny had put the snapshot of Michael and the boy in red bathing trunks in that window.

…

"It's beautiful, dear," Joan Crawford said from Michael's television, on which she had just unveiled an ornamental fawn. "Is it finished?"

"You should know, mother," Diane Baker said. "An artist never knows when she's finished."

The doorbell rang. Michael looked at his watch. It was just after 11:30. He stepped into some gym shorts and leaned out the window. Two floors below, he saw Bobby standing on the front stoop.

"Heads up," he called, dropping the keys in a graceful arc through the fog. There was a laugh below and Michael heard the entrance door slam.

Smiling, he headed for the kitchen to get a couple of beers. As he closed the refrigerator, he heard the front door open and close. "Bobby," he called. "Want a beer?"

The living room was dark and empty. A patch of light fell across the hardwood floor from the bedroom. "These Winnebagos," a loud voice was calling from the television. "We're *giving* 'em away!"

The light in the bedroom went out.

...

Bobby's apartment was dark. A little after 11:30, he stirred slightly in his sleep, huddled on his left side beneath the covers, his face flushed against the paleness of the pillows and the counterpane.

He is standing at the Video Stud terminal. On the screen, the Fireman grins at him, his hands moving teasingly up and down the thick rubber shaft of his hose, which is oozing blobs of fire-fighting foam. He winks at Bobby, foam dripping onto his crotch, soaking his Calvin Klein briefs. "I'm better," the Video Stud Fireman says, letting the now pulsating hose slip to the floor of the set where it continues to throb, expelling periodic spurts of grayish white foam. "I'm much better than him," the Fireman whispers. "Look over at the bar."

Bobby turns. He is standing in the smoky haze of the Drunken Sailor in Baltimore. The jukebox is blaring its Saturday night blare: "You never know how great a kiss can feel, when you stop at the top of a Ferris wheel, when I fell in love . . ."

A tall blond in a letter sweater is moving through the crowd at the end of the bar, followed by a slightly shorter young man. Bobby gasps. He is watching himself leave the Drunken Sailor with Michael. But, in the doorway, the other young man turns and smiles at him. It's Brandy.

"Bobby," says the Video Stud Fireman behind him. "Forget him."

Another record drops into the slot on the jukebox. A waltz in three-quarter time, growing louder and fading only to change again, faltering into pseudoclassical bravura, a low-budget film score. "Bobby," whispers the Video Stud Fireman. "Bobby, look here. See what I've got? It's all yours, Bobby," he sighs.

Bobby turns to the Video Stud terminal.

The Fireman stands naked, framed in a doorway, surrounded with mirrors. Suddenly, there is a flash of stainless steel. The Fireman screams. His body is a package quickly opened, narrow red ribbons flying from the flesh. As the Fireman falls, Bobby pushes through the crowd.

Outside, he rushes through cramped streets, finally coming to a stop and leaning, half-falling, against a filthy brick wall at the end of a block of row houses.

"Kid?" says Michael's Uncle Vernon from the shadow of a crumbling Victorian doorway. "It won't be long now, whether you come along or not." A match flares as he lights a cigar. "You got to know what you want, Bobby," he says. "Me, now. I never did much like Baltimore."

...

Mike Reardon was in his late thirties and had been on the road for a medical supply company for ten years. There were two balloon payments left on his mortgaged home in Milford, Ohio. His wife Dorothy taught Special Ed in Cincinnati and his two children, Larry and Denise, were in the third and fifth grades respectively.

He had a pleasantly rugged face and he kept his body hard with racquetball and Nautilus workouts. On the road, he did an hour of isometrics every morning before breakfast.

Working on the road three weeks out of five helped him keep his life neatly compartmentalized. At home, he was the devoted family man. On the road, he kept to himself and discreetly pursued his only obsession: Youth.

Johnny didn't like them to take him to motels. Particularly in a city like this, where all the motels seemed to be on the desolate outskirts. But this guy had been pleasant, not like some of the pigs he got stuck with. He'd talked to him like he was a friend or a kid brother. Johnny even pretended interest in his display of sample cases with their seemingly endless variety of scalpels, little silver hammers, and gleaming surgical saws sparkling in velvet linings.

And he'd paid him $100 up front.

Johnny hadn't minded wearing the jockstrap and socks and was actually pleasantly surprised when the guy had made him come. Johnny usually had to spit in his hand to fake the come.

92

It was a little after 11:30 and Johnny lay on the big motel bed feeling very mellow. The guy had even provided some Thai stick. In the bathroom, the water went on and he could hear the guy whistling some golden oldie in the shower.

He stretched and rolled over, flipping on the MTV channel.

...

As Michael stood in the darkened living room, the light from the kitchen cast his shadow across the floor and into the bedroom which was lit now only by the television set.

Holding the two cans of cold beer he hesitated. "Bobby?"

There was a low giggle from the bedroom.

"This isn't very funny," Michael said, stepping to the bedroom door.

"Yes it is," said Brandy, curled naked on his bed. His clothes were piled haphazardly on the rattan chair by the television on which Joan Crawford appeared to be having a migraine attack.

"What are you doing here?" said Michael, opening a beer.

"Guess." He stonily smiled a chipped tooth smile. "Do you like my haircut?" he asked. "It's just like Bobby's. See? All the blond's gone."

"Come on," Brandy said, patting the bed and flexing his body. "I've got everything Bobby's got." He giggled. "Even the scar. See?"

"I'm tired," Michael said softly.

"You're not that tired," Brandy smiled, getting up from the bed. "Besides, Bobby isn't here." He put his hands on Michael's waist, hooking one forefinger in the elastic of the gym shorts. "Come on, we can pretend we're in Baltimore."

"How do you know about Baltimore?" Michael said as Brandy worked the shorts down his hips.

"Maybe I dreamed it," Brandy smiled, leading him to the bed.

As Michael entered him, two Joan Crawfords wrestled with a fire ax on the television screen.

. . .

The john, who was apparently taking the longest shower in the history of motels, had left a little mound of change with his car keys on the nightstand. The hand tooled wallet in his Robert Hall suit had contained only a ten dollar bill and some traveler's checks.

Johnny dropped four of the john's quarters into the Massage Away meter. "Yeah," Johnny said, lying on his belly on the undulating bed. "Massage awaaaaay . . ." He lit a cigarette and turned his stoned attention back to the mammoth screen.

The screen was full of sky and some synthesizers vamped a fox trot. "Eeeeee

. . . maaaaah . . . go!" a chorus of voices crooned to the growing frenzy of the synthesizers and an electric guitar. A boy's laughing face jumped up into the frame, wet hair flying wildly for a split second before he fell out of frame again. With three jump cuts, the camera refocussed on the leaping boy in red bathing trunks. With each leap, the trunks slipped lower and he pulled them up with his left hand in midair. His sunburned chest rose and fell with the repetitive music as he leaped into the summer air again and again, his mouth opening and closing in a silent whoop of delight. His hair whipped wet and dark about his joyous face, catching the sunlight.

On the rocking bed, Johnny felt a cold chill. The heavy, sweet scent of lilacs was filling the room.

Behind the leaping, silently whooping boy in the red bathing trunks, in the tangled trees and undergrowth of a fairy tale swamp, something moved furtively, its movements corresponding to the opening and closing of the leaping boy's mouth.

His hands trembling, Johnny flipped the channel selector.

A black and white picture filled the screen, computerized reds, blues, and yellows trying to bleed in at its edges. In a stand of willows smothered in Spanish moss, a gaunt figure loomed, faceless in the dim studio twilight. Slowly, orchestrated by the swelling sound of an autoharp, the camera tracked through thick clouds of Dry Ice, turning, turning, as the triumphant colors overwhelmed the screen.

A golden light burned in the window of a weathered building at the edge of a swamp. The camera crept closer now, peering through that window: A handsome young man looked up, a rapidly snatched towel in his right hand barely obscuring his genitals.

"Must be the adult channel," Mike Reardon laughed, naked in the open doorway of the steam shrouded bathroom.

Johnny screamed.

. . .

Bobby turned on the bathroom light. His face was drawn in the mirror. He was tired all the time. And yet he seemed to be sleeping more than he ever had before. And the dreams . . .

He brushed his teeth vigorously. While he was still a teenager, he had found that the boring reality of toothbrush and toothpaste could do a lot for you in the middle of the night.

Shithead, he thought. You've slept perfectly well without him on and off over the past goddamn decade. He smiled at himself in the mirror, his mouth foaming with toothpaste. And his face froze.

Someone was standing behind him. There, in the darkened room just beyond the door. He could see him in the mirror. The figure stepped forward slightly.

"It's begun," Michael's Uncle Vernon said softly. "Stick to your guns, kid."

When he turned, he faced only empty darkness. When he turned on the lights the room was empty.

...

Brandy lit a cigarette, contentedly tangled in Michael's sleeping body. He caught himself in a giggle. Angel dust always made him giggle.

The room was nice. But there weren't any pictures on the walls. He'd have to get Michael some pictures.

Dreaming beside him, Michael was five years old. It was a late winter afternoon, dark and quiet hovering over the endless fields of crusted snow. Cold was seeping through the baseboards in the living room. He was lying on his stomach on the faded rose carpet, looking at the funny papers.

Jack Armstrong and a woman with flowers in her hair were fleeing a maddened swarm of deadly wasps. The woman was wearing a shiny two-piece dress that exposed her flat belly. Bellybutton, Michael thought. As they raced towards a jungle river, Jack Armstrong tore off his safari jacket and shirt. There was something breathless about his graphically inked chest and arms. As the exhausted woman lost her footing, he swept her into his arms, hardly breaking stride. Michael stared at the expanses of funny paper flesh, Jack Armstrong's arms and chest, the woman's soft and exposed belly, for long moments, feeling slightly dizzy.

He felt like he had to go to the bathroom and his ears were ringing.

With a shout, Jack Armstrong wrapped the woman in his shirt and jacket and leaped off the cliff into the alligator infested river.

Brandy stretched, letting his flank slide along Michael's. Michael's breathing altered slightly and, in his sleep, he turned more fully against him. Brandy smiled. There was a lot of night left.

Distracted by the warm flesh sliding against his own, Michael sighed, his eyes still closed, and stretched. The familiar animal warmth creeping along his belly sent Jack Armstrong and the bare bellied woman hurtling back through the years into the oblivion from which they had wandered only dreaming moments ago.

With a throaty laugh, Michael rolls towards the nameless warmth beside him: There is nothing there but cold and damp.

Framed by the rust torn screen of the north attic window, a hangman's moon floats in a colorless sky. Pallid light falls in three ragged bars across the old brass bed where portions of the ceiling have collapsed. The sopping mattress is rank with mold, strewn with the dead leaves that are scattered everywhere.

He slides off the bed, his flesh clammy, smeared with the decay that has overtaken the weather-beaten bedding. Ruined boards threaten to give beneath his weight. Here and there, the floor is gone, rotting wood sagging from the weather stained joists. There is the furtive scampering of vermin in the darkest corners.

...

Brandy turned on his side carefully so that Michael's body was still pressed against him and looked at the television. On the screen, a young man in jeans and a bomber jacket turned to face him.

...

From the ruined bannister, Michael hears a downstairs door open on rusty hinges. Through the gaping floorboards, shafts of lamplight reach for the remnants of the ceiling. Above the stairs to the left, the light escapes the room, climbing through the gnarled and leafless branches of a dying silver birch, spreading through the wisps of fog only to be swallowed by the endless darkness that divides the earth from the stars.

There are footsteps in the parlor below. Dragging sounds. Wordless whispers.

...

Brandy frowned. The show on the television was weird. Or maybe it was the angel dust.

"It comes as a shock, let me tell you," the young man on the screen said, laughing. "But there are these open doors?" Smiling, he took off his bomber jacket and started to unbutton his shirt. "And sleeping beauty there is one of them." He tossed off his shirt and started to undo his belt. "Astral doorways," he laughed, unbuttoning his faded jeans. "Far out, huh?" He bent slightly at the waist, never taking his eyes from Brandy's, stepping out of the jeans. "You don't look anything like the kid I'm looking for," he said. "But I've got all the time in the world," he winked, sliding cotton briefs down his long legs. "Let's pretend that my name is Captain Masters, okay?" He gave his sex a long, lingering pull. "And you, let's pretend that your name is Eve . . ."

...

At his hotel, Johnny had packed his rucksack quickly, knowing that he couldn't use the car for long. By the time he hit the interstate he was calmer. The john had asked for a wakeup call at 6. That left him at least four hours, probably even more before the car was reported missing.

It was a little red Volvo. He had told Michael once that he had a little red Volvo. "It's in the shop," he had said. "See?" he said to the rearview mirror. "I *do* have a little red Volvo." He smiled. "For awhile."

He wondered if Michael was still mad at him. When he dreamed of Michael, he always felt safe. He tried to dream of Michael as often as possible, because when Michael was beside him, he knew he was safe, even if Michael was asleep. If he was sleeping with Michael, maybe the awful dreams wouldn't keep coming.

The little red Volvo had been heading east for the past quarter-hour. Maybe Michael wasn't mad at him anymore. Taking one hand from the wheel, he felt in his jeans for the only keys he had.

The little clock on the dash said 2:45. Three hours and fifteen minutes. He started looking for a turnaround. He couldn't drive all the way, of course. And maybe something better would come along. But what was the point of heading east?

He smiled and turned up the radio.

...

In his brightly lit bedroom, beneath blankets twisted high as those of a frightened child, Bobby thinks at first that he is wandering the crumbling old pier again. But, as he turns towards the shore, he realizes the rotten wood beneath his feet is only a narrow wooden walkway and not a pier at all. He is surrounded by marsh grass and willows. Thick ground fog ebbs and flows on the stagnant swamp water that surrounds him.

His feet sliding on the damp and rotten wood, he picks his way carefully towards a clearing in the trees and undergrowth where an arc of golden light sprawls across a weed-tangled yard.

There are furtive sounds in the dense undergrowth, occasional splashing in the fetid water. Drifting in the distance, music waltzes in three-quarter time across the shallows from the open water and beyond.

"Got bigger, didn't you, Johnny?" the bloated thing in rotting coveralls whispers in his ear, flaking, grey fleshed arms pinning him from behind. "Bigger," it wheezes, "but no smarter and no faster."

...

The young man, his tanned flesh backlit by the television set, stood by the bed now. Brandy stared up at him, motionless.

"Why don't you ask me?" the young man laughed.

Brandy's eyes smarted. Angel dust or no angel dust, he wasn't going to start talking to someone who had just stepped out of a television set.

"Let me fuck you," the young man whispered. "Don't you want to be an astral doorway?" He smiled, putting one cold palm on Brandy's trembling shoulder.

"Wouldn't you like that?"

...

Flattened against the blistered wallpaper of the north attic wall, Michael can hear it in the distance: music waltzing across the shallows, through the stand of willows, rushing in three-quarter time from the dust and cobwebs of the deserted hotel where the last guest had checked out more than a decade ago.

Downstairs, the sounds are more furtive now, the whispers more indistinct. Shadows thrown by the lamplight through the gaping floorboards move slowly across the ruined beams and ragged patches of roof above him.

There is a creaking sound at the foot of the stairwell, a scraping at the damp-swollen door. When the rust-frozen latch refuses to turn, Michael's heart beats two loud beats in the sudden silence.

A car horn beeps three times in the yard. Turning to the north attic window, Michael sees the old Nash in the weed-choked yard, its headlights cutting a path of golden light to the ruined side porch beneath him.

Scrambling onto the loose shingles of the porch roof, he hears the attic door groan open and there is a soft sigh in the darkness behind him. There is the odor of dust and rotting velvet. That and something else—stale, sharp, and vaguely feral.

The door on the driver's side of the old Nash opens, and in the courtesy light Michael can see Aunt Vivian looking up at him.

Behind him, there is a rustling, a sound of dead leaves and rotting fabric and there is sudden laughter, ripe and brutal, the barking of hyenas.

He is about to look behind him when Aunt Vivian calls from the sloping ground below him, gesturing angrily in the headlights.

"Will you look alive, Mikie? Wake up! This is not some Saturday matinee movie show here. Jump!"

...

With a crooked smile, the young man straddled Brandy, his weight pressing Brandy into the mattress, his tanned flesh radiating cold.

Although he could think of nothing to say, Brandy wanted to speak. Somehow, this wasn't pleasant. He wanted to move, but in the growing cold he could barely breathe. Staring up into the young man's face, it occurred to Brandy that there was something about the young man that wasn't as attractive at close range.

Then he noticed them. Thin lines that crisscrossed the young man's forehead, running through his cheeks. Thin, white lines. There were others on his neck and torso, a fine tracery of very thin white lines in the tanned flesh. As Brandy stared at them, they seemed to grow deeper, pulsing slightly.

Then Brandy tried to close his eyes. He didn't want to see this, man . . .

And then, Michael was grabbing him and he screamed twice. It felt very good to scream. "The television, man!" he shuddered into Michael's chest.

Michael looked at the television over Brandy's quaking shoulders. A man in a chef's hat was offering late night viewers a special deal on a set of knives sharp enough to slice wood. "As if it was *butter!*" the fat man smiled.

"It was just a dream," Michael whispered. Dream. The word seemed to echo in the overheated room.

"Bummer," Brandy sighed. "Bummer, bummer, bummer . . ."

...

There was a whine in Bobby's ears, the sounds of birds frying on a high-tension wire. The darkness was receding. He was in his own bedroom, face down on the bed. The lights were still on. His face pressed into the pillows, he could see the wall three feet in front of his face. He could see the wall perfectly. He couldn't move. But he could feel.

He could feel the covers being yanked off him.

"Now," the guttural voice wheezed just behind him. "You gonna be nice or am I gonna have to make it rough?" Bobby saw its shadow on the wall in front of his unblinking eyes. A hulking silhouette. "Up to you," it wheezed. "Nasty or nice."

The bed groaned and weight pressed against the length of his body. He could feel it. It was squirming full-length against him. With one knee it pried his legs apart. "Nice, Johnny," it wheezed. "Gonna give it to you nice, now."

It swept over him in thick, pungent waves. An odor of mold, damp, sour, and spoiled. And smoke. Cigar smoke.

"Move, kid," Michael's Uncle Vernon said from a far corner of the room. "Move! That's all it takes."

There was a coarse grunt, a final thrust, and Bobby came up on both elbows.

He was alone. The mechanical whine was gone.

...

Johnny's mouth was dry and his eyes felt gritty. "Sandman's coming," Mommy used to say to him and Tommy when they didn't want to go to bed yet. "Sandman's going to shovel sand in your eyes!" He and Tommy used to have nightmares about the Sandman.

Poor Mommy. Except at the phone company, Mommy never knew how to do shit. He wondered if Mommy was still in Arizona. Maybe someday he would look her up. One of his sisters had a snapshot of Mommy on a run-down porch. She was wearing a housedress with big flowers on it. "Hi, Mommy," he would say. "Long time no see . . ."

In a pig's ass. He watched another Indian reservation slip past. He wished he was still driving. He'd made good time last night, almost four-hundred miles. He'd left the little red Volvo in a deserted Tastee Freeze lot well over the Kansas line.

Fucking buses. They take forever.

He took out the alligator wallet and flipped through the snapshots again, as he always did when he was bored. He looked at the new one. He wasn't sure why he'd kept it. But it had been the only one of interest in the hand tooled wallet.

A very young Mike Reardon smiled through the plastic at Johnny. Tan, laughing in a pair of old cutoffs, he looked a good deal leaner than he had last night. On the back, in faded letters: "July, 1965, Horseheads. Trip with Randy."

Pocketing the wallet, Johnny yawned. Weird. He started to drift to sleep again.

With a little silver hammer, Johnny plays a tune on Tommy's toy xylophone. Tommy, he calls. Tommy? Look what I got . . .

In his hip pocket, the snapshots dreamed as well.

. . .

In the breakfast nook, Bobby pours himself another cup of coffee. Sunlight is streaming through the windows. It seems impossible in daylight. And yet the dirty sheets are in the hamper.

In the steam shrouded morning mirror, he had seen the bruises. And . . .

"It's 10:15 on a beautiful morning here at KZAP and we have a request coming up," an overly coked disc jockey mellows into his microphone. "This one is for you, Bobby," the voice croons. "A real oldie from your old buddy, K.C., who says he's sorry he missed you last night."

"Last night I took a walk after dark," sings the radio. "I went down to Palisades Park to see what I could seeeeeee . . ."

Bobby smiles. It must be some other Bobby's favorite oldie. He doesn't know any K.C.

". . . eeeeeeeeeeeeeeeeeeeeee . . ." the harsh syllable wavers from a single, battered groove until it blends into static.

"Technical difficulties," a husky voice whispers from the radio. "But we'll overcome them, Bobby. You're gonna be mine. Wait'll you see what I got, babe." There is a sharp, smooth intake of breath. "And it's all gonna be yours, Bobby. Hear me, babe? ALL YOURS!!!"

". . . kiss can feel, when you stop at the top of a Ferris wheel, when I fell in love . . ."

The song blares from the bright yellow Motorola with the round blue dial. The same radio that Bobby was given for Christmas when he was seven years old. Every Saturday morning, he used to turn on the little Motorola in his room and listen to "Big Jon and Sparky," and "The Land of the Lost," and "Sky King."

Even though it didn't work that well anymore, he had taken the Motorola with him to Baltimore. It had set on top of the refrigerator in the apartment he and Michael had shared for three years in Baltimore.

It had somehow gotten lost when they had moved. The Motorola had been lost long before he lost Michael's letter sweater.

Numbly, Bobby lights a cigarette. The Motorola is on the refrigerator.

"Welcome," says the high-pitched voice on the little radio, "to The Land of the Lost."

...

Brandy rolls onto his side, yawning into the pillow. In another room, he can hear the radio blaring some kid's program. Beside him, Michael mumbles something about Italian meatless ravioli and starts to snore.

Brandy reaches for his pack of cigarettes on the nightstand. The old brass bed creaks beneath him. There is no nightstand. His cigarettes are on a wooden chair next to the bed. His and Michael's clothing is piled on another bed. There are three other beds in the room, all as large and old as the one he and Michael are lying in.

Warm air is drifting down from the weather stained ceiling, soaking in from the tarpaper roof. Through the torn green shades the morning sun shimmers in dusty streamers across warped wooden floorboards.

On the other side of a musty stairwell, a silver-webbed mirror throws flickering sunlight in twisting patterns on the sloping ceiling.

Brandy knows he didn't go to sleep here. He has never even seen this room before.

Bummer, Brandy thinks. His hands shake as he lights a cigarette.

…

In his torn green bathrobe, Bobby is sitting on one of the two chrome and cracked plastic chairs that match the chrome and Formica kitchen table in the apartment he and Michael used to share in Baltimore.

The kitchen is bright with thick coats of cheap yellow paint with orange trim. Both Michael and he had hated it enough to repeatedly agree to repaint the room. Someday.

He stands. Through the half-open window over the sink he can see Arcadia Street, narrow, cobblestoned, pressed in by its leaning row houses. The gauzy curtains stir in a breeze heavy with magnolias and exhaust.

He walks across the room and opens the door into the small back bedroom. On the unmade bed, Michael's jeans and a fresh shirt are laid out. His underpants lay crumpled on the floor with Bobby's, in passive communion with several pairs of socks.

Bobby thinks of laboratory rats running through mazes. He thinks of the tiny electrodes stitched beneath their little shaved scalps.

"This time," the Motorola sings behind him, "we're really breaking up . . . This time is for-evvv-er . . ."

…

"What?" says Brandy. "All you can say is 'what'? Jesus Christ," he mutters, trying to extract his underpants from the pile of clothing. "Some psycho comes out of the television and feels me up and then tries to fucking *bleed* all over me, for Christ's sake—fucking disgusting—and you say 'Calm down, calm down, it's only a dream, it's only a dream'. Okay, okay, okay, I say. Wonderful. So you fuck me again, which part, really, is okay by me, and we go back to sleep. Nice." He stumbles into his underpants. "Now this? Bummer," Brandy sighs. "Bummer, man. Heavy bummer."

"We're at the lake," Michael says softly.

"The lake?" Brandy looks at him, hands on his hips. "Great. The lake. What fucking lake? And how did we get here?"

"I don't know," Michael sighs, still not moving.

"You don't know. Fabulous." Fuming, he dresses quickly, ripping his shirt in the process. "You gonna just lay there or what?"

"Something's wrong," says Michael.

"What was your first clue?"

"Brandy . . ."

"Look," Brandy says, turning towards the stairs. "Get dressed, okay? I mean, do something, okay? Now I'm gonna . . . I'm gonna go downstairs and try to figure out where the hell we are. Okay?"

Michael slowly swings his legs over the edge of the bed. Below him, he hears Brandy open the latch on the door.

"Oh man," Brandy whimpers from the bottom of the stairwell. "Oh man. This is . . . Oh shit, man. Bummer City." He begins to cry.

. . .

Pulling on a pair of dungarees, Bobby hears:

"Mister?" a kid's voice calls from Arcadia Street. "Mister? I can't find the door."

The door was always by the refrigerator. But now there is no door. Blank walls . . . He looks out the window. The kid is standing on the strip of lawn between the sidewalk and the window.

"Can I come in, mister?" the kid asks in an excited voice. "I'm lost and I want to call my mom."

"Sure," Bobby says. "But . . ."

"You look kind of scared, mister," says the kid. "Can't you find the door, either?"

Bobby just stares at the kid.

"Don't you live here?"

"I . . . I used to," Bobby says.

"Are you lost, too?"

Bobby nods.

"Can I climb in the window?" the kid asks. "If I can climb in the window and call my mom, maybe she can come and get both of us."

...

Beyond the door at the foot of the crooked stairs, yesterday's dust settles softly in the cramped room, colorless and final as the faded fleurs-de-lys on the walls. A pillow has tumbled soundlessly to the floor beside the rumpled bed. In the corner, the battered radiator releases an exhausted sigh.

On the far wall, the goddess in her dime store frame turns her head slowly towards him. "Careful," she whispers sadly, her breath slightly misting the cracked glass imprisoning her. She smiles her sweet, defeated smile. "People like you and me, Brandy, when we dial 911, they put us on hold."

Brandy turns around, his face ashen.

Halfway up the stairs, Michael looks down at him sleepily. He is dressed in Roy Rogers pajamas. He is six years old.

"Who are you?" he asks.

There is a ragged teddy bear dangling from Michael's right hand. "Maybe tomorrow night," the teddy bear whispers, leaking sawdust. "Maybe that's when he'll get you."

...

The kid clambers down from the window sill to the drainboard of the sink. Hunching down, he swings his legs off the enameled edge and, gracefully clumsy as a kitten's, his sneaker-shod feet land on the linoleum.

He smiles at Bobby for a moment and then looks down at his sneakers. The right one has come untied. Frowning, he bends down to tie it.

"Thanks, mister," he smiles up from the floor. "For inviting me in."

"Sure," says Bobby. Something about the kid's smile . . .

"My name is Kenneth Charles Cooper," the kid says softly. "But you can call me K.C."

Bobby steps back a few steps. "The phone . . ." he says.

"The phone?" smiles the kid.

"You want to use the phone."

"Oh," says the kid. "Do I?"

As he laughs, a sudden raven's wing of blackness sweeps through the room. "Thumbelina, Thumbelina," a chorus of children's voices sings from the bottomless well of dark. "Pretttt-ttty litttt-ttttle thing . . ."

...

With a shudder, Brandy came up on his left elbow. Michael's sleeping body was draped half across his, cutting off the circulation in his right arm and leg, both of which were limp and weak.

Carefully, he extracted himself from Michael's warm limbs. Lighting a cigarette, he padded quietly into the kitchen. The sun was shining brightly in the breakfast nook. On the table were a Daffy Duck mug and bowl, a box of Cheerios, and a tin foil packet of hot chocolate.

Brandy yawned and filled a pan with water, looking for matches.

...

Michael gets up from the edge of the sway-backed brass bed and steps to the railing. The door at the foot of the stairway is standing open. "Brandy?" he calls.

There is no answer. In the silence, he can hear the sound of a motorboat in the distance. From the back of a limping chair, he takes an old flannel bathrobe of Uncle Vernon's, tying the green and brown checkered belt as he descends the steep and crooked stairs.

The shades are drawn in the parlor. A dog-eared paperback western, *Shootout at the Dream Corral,* lies open on the faded linoleum by the horsehair rocker. On the long side table, beside a yellowing pile of *Planet Stories* and *Ranch Romances,* Aunt Vivian's dentures smile at him from a Hopalong Cassidy tumbler.

He pulls up the green shade on one of the front windows. The twin silver beeches and lilacs are no longer there. Peering through the dusty glass, Michael can see the breakfast nook in his kitchen. On the table are a Daffy Duck mug and bowl, a box of Cheerios, and a tin foil packet of hot chocolate. There are three balloons taped to the edge of the table, on the very center of which is a cake with the greeting "welcome home, Johnny!" written on it in blood red icing. Surrounding the cake are several packages wrapped in colored tissue paper.

A young man in jeans and a bomber jacket walks into the kitchen and waves at Michael, smiling. He puts an open straight razor with a blue ribbon tied to its handle on the table.

Michael stands silently in Uncle Vernon's bathrobe as the young man walks around the table to the window. His arms embrace the window frame and his face looms forward, nearly touching the glass. His smile grows sweeter, his half-closed eyes only inches from Michael's. His lips open and a patch of the window steams up from his breath. With his right forefinger the young man writes on the misted glass: "This is from me"

...

Bobby lay on his back, sunlight streaming in the bedroom windows. He felt the dreams slipping away and stretched, feeling lame and tired. With a yawn and a cough, he pulled on his green bathrobe and went into the kitchen.

It was well after noon. He flipped on the radio and turned to the sink, the battered kettle in one hand.

On the drainboard was a small muddy sneaker print.

"Never," sang the radio, "Never, ever . . . No, I'll never, never, never . . . dance again . . . No, no, no, no, I'll never . . ."

. . .

"It's after noon," Brandy smiled down at Michael, kneeling on the bed. "I've got a surprise," he said, vaulting up and taking a tray from the dresser. "Breakfast in bed," he smiled, placing the tray on Michael's lap.

"What . . .?" Michael said sleepily, looking down at the tray.

"I knew just what you wanted," Brandy said. "Cause you already had it all laid out."

Michael stared at the Cheerios in the Daffy Duck bowl, the cocoa in the Daffy Duck mug.

"Me," said Brandy, slipping back beneath the covers and taking a coffee cup from the tray, "I'm just having coffee. With lots of sugar." He smiled. "Chocolate, man, it makes me break out something awful."

IV

It is getting to be lunchtime on a bright, warm day in late June and Kenneth Charles Cooper is running up Academy Street. Gosh, he thinks, this is the greatest day in my life!

He and Chatty Whitmore are making their own 3-D comic book! They have a huge pack of newsprint that they bought from Marciel Bishop down at the Pennysaver for only 25 cents and they each have a pencil that's blue on one end and red on the other that Chatty's mom gave them. For two weeks now they've been saving up shirt cardboards to make the 3-D glasses frames. And they're going to make the lenses out of the cellophane off milk bottles. The red comes on whole milk and the blue comes on skim milk. So the 3-D glasses won't cost them a cent!

Chatty has his own little red stapler that came in a school kit he got last year. And he already has four and a half boxes of staples, so their whole investment is only 25 cents! After lunch, K.C. is going back down to Chatty's and they're going to start drawing. They already have a great story all figured out. It's going to be called Treadmill of the Dreaming Dead!

The heroes are going to be named Captain Armstrong Chatmore and Captain Kansas City Cooper! And they're going to have great costumes, too!

When K.C. and Chatty are done, they'll be the richest and most famous guys in the seventh grade!

Chatty has some really great ideas! But Chatty says that K.C. has the very best ones! That's because K.C. has all these really great dreams.

Like the one last night! This neat old man and woman came up to his bedroom where he was sleeping and asked him to go find this friend of their nephew! And then he was walking down this funny street that was all bricks and then this guy invited him into this house that didn't have a door!

K.C. is having neat dreams like that a lot now. And sometimes, they're even better! They're a little scary, but they'll make great ideas for Treadmill of the Dreaming Dead. *Because in these other dreams, K.C. is all grown up and he's tall and handsome and he keeps having all these adventures!*

Except he can hardly ever remember them in the morning.

DEADLINE

At the edge of a small park the Church of Old Souls stood deserted as it always was in midweek, its congregation now reduced to a handful of parishioners. At the foot of the concrete stairs, dead leaves whispered litanies to the sluggish breeze that moved them fretfully beneath the jimmied window. In the basement, damp, gray light washed through the dusty panes of glass, drizzling down the high stone walls.

Behind the heavy crates, Johnny lay huddled in his sleeping bag. Early in the morning, long before first light, he had walked from the bus station to Michael's apartment building. He had stood on the stoop, his shadow on the orderly line of metal mailboxes, the double row of buzzers, the shiny brass plate that hoped to discourage peddlers.

He had put the key in the entry door and thrown the tumbler. Standing in the lobby, he had looked at the faded floral carpet and smelled the dust. He had thought of Michael sleeping on the floor above him. He had thought of undressing so very quietly and sliding naked into the bed. Soundlessly, his hands would slip along Michael's warm flesh. He would groan in his sleep and by the time he awoke, Johnny would be impaled on his strongest weakness. "Hi," Johnny would say huskily, working his hips just a little faster now. "Long time no see."

He had laughed softly, feeling the warmth stirring in his groin. And then he had caught sight of himself in the full-length mirror.

"Not now," his reflection had told him. "Not when you look so tired and shabby." His reflection had smiled and shook its head. "You want to look like a million bucks, Johnny," it had said. "Do you want him to think you came back because there wasn't any other place to go? Do you want him to know the truth?"

. . .

In the damp darkness of that morning, as Johnny stood in the lobby below, Michael shifted slightly, his mouth moving, moist and soundless against Bobby's sleeping chest:

Flat on his back he can see the shadows on the ceiling cast by the moonlight filtering through the venetian blinds. In the front room, he hears a key turn in the lock and the door whispers open. Quiet, measured footsteps, cautious. Or stealthy . . .

Michael turns onto his side. The young man lying beside him is not Bobby. It is the young man who had written "This is from me" on the misted glass. His bomber jacket is hanging on the back of the rattan chair. His jeans are in a rumpled heap on the floor. His underwear is tangled on the covers.

Michael hears a faint footfall on the bedroom carpet behind him. He starts to look over his shoulder, but he can't move. He can only stare, unblinking at the naked young man stretched out beside him.

In the room behind him someone is undressing quietly. He can see his shadow on the wall beyond the bed. The shadow is moving now as the figure comes around the foot of the bed. As he moves into Michael's line of vision to stand looking down at the naked young man, Michael recognizes him.

Johnny.

Michael watches, motionless, as Johnny climbs onto the bed, straddling the sleeper beside him. He is smiling. His hands caress the sleeper's belly. The sleeper moans softly, arching his back slightly and, with a deep sigh, Johnny repositions himself slightly. The sleeper groans as Johnny's warm flesh engulfs him. The bed is swaying rhythmically now. The sleeper moans again, a long, wild sound, and his eyes come open, shining in the half-light, "Hi," Johnny whispers, riding him frantically now. "Long time no see."

Gleaming. Red ribbons shining through sudden darkness.

...

Bobby, warm against Michael on that slate gray early morning, was breathing evenly, deeply. On his own. But not alone:

Surrounded by rushing, milling strangers clutching plaster mermaids and celluloid kewpie dolls, he has sawdust in his shoes. The kid is clutching his hand.

The kid tugs at his jacket. "Let's go in there," he says, peering through the crowd at the luridly painted broadsides: "See! Captain Masters and Eve! See! The Slaves of the Evil Dead! See! The Corral of Dreams! See! The Fireman and His Big Hose!" the canvas calls through a dusty breeze, thick with rancid grease and Calliope music.

In the line ahead of them, Hitler and Eva Braun secure their tickets. Behind them, the line grows: The Alligator Man, the Human Pincushion, the Siamese

Twins, and Eeeka the Wild Girl, who is carrying a plaster mannikin arm splashed with red paint and wrapped in the crumpled remains of the Sunday funnies.

"No . . ." Bobby mumbles.

The kid smiles up at him. "No?" He shakes his head slowly. "But it's my treat," he whispers. "See?" He holds out his hand. There are two quarters in his sweaty palm.

They are moving now, the crowd behind him growing, jostling and impatient, murmuring.

"Four bits," says the boy in red bathing trunks from behind the little grill in his ticket booth. Smiling a slightly gap-toothed smile, he shakes his wet mane of hair and hitches up his trunks, tearing two large tickets from his roll.

Inside the tent, the bleachers are almost full. Through the scratchy speakers, children sing loudly, "Thumbelina dance! Thumbelina sing!"

The lights are going down now and Bobby shudders. "It's all right," the kid smiles as darkness overtakes them. "I'll hold your hand."

At the thunderous roll of a kettledrum, a flyblown light explodes against a sagging canvas screen: a blurred double image, one red, one blue.

"Here," the kid says, pressing against Bobby's side. "It'll help you see better."

He pulls a lopsided strip of cardboard from his jacket. It is folded in two places in the shape of sunglasses. Two asymmetric holes in the cardboard have red and blue cellophane glued to them with library paste.

"See?" the kid says, putting on a second pair himself. "The longer you look, the better it gets."

Shifted by the colored cellophane, the images on the screen form a temporary alliance and the scene leaps forward at Bobby, suffocating in its closeness.

"See?" the kid whispers, squeezing Bobby's sweaty hand.

A darkened room. On the bed, Bobby sees himself lying motionless. Beside him is Michael.

"Ashes, ashes," the children sing. "All fall down!"

Michael's eyes come open in an expressionless face. Naked, he gets out of bed and wanders forward, closer, closer, closer, his artificially projected three-dimensional flesh hanging in space—as close to Bobby's face as the flesh of his forehead is close to the frontal bone of his skull.

Slowly, the body that Bobby knows in many ways better than his own begins to change. Its coarse hair, its face and pores are softening. The muscles are becoming subtly suppler. Its heavy sex grows lighter, its testicles pull up from a shrinking scrotum, the droop of its penis folds in upon itself until it barely protrudes from its smooth and hairless belly.

And now, its size is diminishing, rapid millimeter by rapid millimeter. Smooth, small, shining, a lost toy is found in the shifting golden light—flickering dim and bright as a seventh Christmas, whispers of a vanished world of occasional puddles, of spilled milk on warm flannel.

A waltz in three-quarter time drifts through the speakers and the Toy Soldier turns and returns with it, this music, glides with it, this warm waltz of sweeter longing and so much softer tears. Once hero of children long grown—and one-two-three, one-two-three, turning again, and turning again—and now: *the warped wooden door . . .*

. . .

Brandy wolfed down the last of a buttermilk doughnut at the All Night Dough Knot on the ragged end of his street. He caught sight of himself in the mirror on the yellow tiled wall. His face was pinched and there were circles under his eyes. The open-all-night lighting didn't help matters much. He hadn't been able to sleep well since the night spent at Michael's.

Fuck, man, he thought, looking at the mirror gloomily. And now my fucking goddamn fucking face is breaking out again. Another doughnut probably wouldn't help.

He left the tepid coffee in its plastic container on the counter and started down the street.

"Babe," someone called from the shadows of a blasted phone booth. "Looking for some action?"

Brandy felt a prickling at the back of his neck as the young man stepped into the street, strangled neon splashing in the puddles of curdled water at his feet. He was tall and well built and there was a vague sweetness to his smile that no more matched his words than it matched his eyes, which were cold and dead.

"Missed you, babe," he smiled. He idly rubbed his chest and belly, which were framed by his dark, unbuttoned shirt.

...

In the crowded tent, as the Toy Soldier opens a warped wooden door, the applause and cheers from the bleachers is deafening. Dusty klieg followspots strafe the audience, catching the howling throng: There are Hitler and Eva Braun, and Bobby Franks holding the Lindberg baby. Here is Eeeka the Wild Girl, holding the battered mannikin arm aloft. Beside her a pallid sailor laughs uncontrollably, his bloated face much paler than the torn flesh and gristle of the empty shoulder socket in the ruin of his midshipman's blouse.

"Bobby," the kid whispers beside him. "The Toy Soldier's here, Bobby. Right out of Uncle Teddy's Storybook." His eyes and teeth gleam in the gloom. "I gotta go now," he whispers. "Gotta grow up now."

The darkness reels around Bobby and now he is lying on his back on the rumpled bed on the canvas stage set. One by one, shadowy forms file through the open doorway, each pausing for a moment at the foot of the bed, staring down at him as if paying their last respects.

Their shapes, like the features on their starved and sallow faces, seem to shift constantly, uncertain what form to take in the harsh and sawdust spangled light. One tries sluggishly to become Michael's Aunt Vivian, its dead eyes staring as its mouth slowly slips in confusion around a cigar and a gray and white moustache half sprouts on its withered upper lip. The bloated thing from the swamp is here, shambling past, too torpid to attempt more human form.

And still they come, faceless now until:

The Video Stud Fireman stands framed in the ruined doorway. "Bobby," he whispers, bright flesh glistening wetly in the flood of shapeless dark eddying around him.

"Thumbelina, Thumbelina," the children's voices swell on the scratchy speakers as the Video Stud Fireman comes closer, carried forward on the dark tide from beyond the door.

"Bobby, look here," he smiles. His torso flexes. Once. Twice. Flowing with the obsidian waves. "See what I've got?" he sighs, body rippling with the waves, surging as flesh and muscle never can, anchored as they are to bone and tendon. "It's all yours, Bobby." The words stream from his mouth, wet with shadow, seeping from slack lips.

The crowd in the bleachers stands, its voices joining the high, sweet, sexless song of the children on the dusty speakers.

Flesh slides towards Bobby, shape slipping against shape, an engorged

Hollywood dream of full moons and hairy palms.

Bobby starts to scream.

"Thumbelina dance," sings Bobby Franks. Sing Adolph and Eva. "Thumbelina sing," sings Sharon Tate. Sing Eeeka and the savaged sailor . . .

. . .

Michael stretched and turned the pillow, exhausted and tense. He had been lying quietly, slightly curled on his left side, but the sleep that still held Bobby in its thrall had deserted him.

With a sigh, he got out of bed. He was just through the door into the living room when the kitchen light went on. He heard the cupboard doors open and a faucet splashed water into the sink.

"Hi, Mikie," the kid said brightly, in the slightly superior way older kids take with their juniors. "Did you have a bad dream?" He took a big swallow of water from a tumbler. "Want some?" he asked, wiping his mouth with the back of one hand, offering Michael the half-full tumbler with the other.

Michael took the glass, It seemed very large in his hand.

"Here," the kid said, slipping off his wool bathrobe. "You'll catch cold like that." He handed Michael the bathrobe, "What happened to your PJ's?" He smiled. "Did you wet the bed?"

. . .

Brandy turned the corner, out of breath. Shit, man, he thought, his heart

pounding his ribs, get it together, get it together . . . The guy had only wanted
to score. It happens every night. Face it, it's a compliment, Brandy thought.
I mean, face it, you know you aren't a scumbag, right? Even if you are getting
a few zits.

The eyes. The fucking eyes, man! And those marks—like that fucking dream,
man . . . Bum yourself out, why don't you? Go all out, huh? What, you never
heard of drugs? That's all it was, poor fucker all cranked up or down. Might
have even been a so-so fuck. So what's the big deal? Guy takes some pills,
can't sleep, wants to make the piggy with two backs, what the fuck, right?

"Excuse me," called a man behind the wheel of a red Volvo idling at the curb.
"Do you know the way to 101 south?"

"It's . . ." Brandy looked down the street. The guy with the weird eyes had just
turned onto the rain and oil slicked pavement at the corner. "If you give me
a lift," Brandy said suddenly, his heart racing again, "I can show you." He
swallowed hard as the passenger door swung open. "I don't live far from the
on-ramp," he said.

"Just throw the cases in the back," said the man. He smiled. "Medical supplies."

"Yeah?" said Brandy, sliding onto the cool leather seat. "Doc, huh?"

"Salesman. Boring," he said, stepping on the accelerator. "Tell me about yourself,
babe," he smiled. "I bet you're not boring." He patted Brandy's knee. "You
can call me the Salesman." The hand slid slightly, coming to rest against

Brandy's thigh.

"My name's Brandy," said Brandy. "And you can go right ahead, man."

"What?" said the Salesman.

"Feel up my crotch, too," Brandy sighed. "What the hell, you know? Everybody does it." Yeah, Brandy thought. I'm the fucking Playmate of the Month tonight. Regular Matt Dillon of the zits here . . .

"Look, I didn't mean . . ."

"Of course not," sighed Brandy. "Nobody ever does."

"Look," the Salesman said. "Maybe we could go to a motel."

"Yeah," said Brandy. "Maybe we could get married and go to Vegas for our honeymoon, too, right? And someday you can sue me for custody of the kids."

"Are you pissed off?"

"Pissed off? Me? What reason have I got to be pissed off, man?" He shook his head. "Wow, man, I should be so lucky every night, right? Like, out of fucking gratitude I should blow you right here in the passing lane, right?"

"Music?" the Salesman asked softly, his hand moving from Brandy's lap to the radio dials.

Brandy's eyes felt heavy. They were filled with sand. The tires hummed on the rainy pavement as the voice on the radio said:

"A heavy storm front towards Wichita . . ."

Fucking Wichita? Brandy thought. And then he was asleep.

. . .

The green night light that Uncle Vernon had made for him lit the little room softly, a hazy beacon on a blue dresser cluttered with toys and picture books. Mickey Mouse, Donald Duck, the Little Red Hen, and Batman and Robin guarded the room from the walls on which Aunt Vivian had painted them.

"Here," the kid said. "Back in your jammies." He knelt down and slipped one of Michael's little legs and then another into the Dr. Dentons. With a laugh, he slid Michael into bed, pulling the covers up to his chin.

"Where's Aunt Vivian?" Michael asked in a small child's voice.

"She and Uncle Vernon are gone," the kid said, sitting on the edge of the tiny bed and ruffling Michael's cowlicks. "I'm going to take care of you now." He smiled a very serious and adult smile.

"Where did they go?"

"Shhh," the kid whispered. "If you promise to go back to sleep now, I'll tell you a story."

Michael looked at him gravely, one thumb wandering between his lips.

"Remember the toy soldier and the plastic mouse?"

Michael furrowed his brow and shook his little head, sucking his thumb in earnest now.

"Well," the kid said, "this one is about the toy soldier and the dead boy." The room seemed much darker now. And cold. Very cold. "Once upon a time, while looking for his heart, the toy soldier remembered his best friend in all the world, a little dead boy. He had been looking for his heart everywhere. And he had grown very tired. Sometimes he would think he had found it. But he had found a different part of his body instead. A very different part, indeed . . ."

. . .

Brandy shivered awake against the steamy window as the rainy night highway, rutted and narrow, snaked past beneath the overheated Volvo. This wasn't 101.

Sleepy. Fucking sleepy.

"It isn't far," the Salesman said.

"What isn't far?" Brandy said, motionless against the door.

"My motel," he said.

The land was flat and desolate in every direction. Traffic was sparse, but industrial smoke hid the moon and stars. Broken neon sputtered in the darkness in every direction. The land was blasted and barren.

Another planet, Brandy thought. It could be another planet.

...

Sweating, Bobby rolled over, reaching out for Michael. Michael's side of the bed was empty. The wet night still pressed against the steam shrouded windows. Still groggy, he leaned on one elbow, rubbing his eyes. And he felt something brush against his leg. Cold with a rush of adrenaline he looked towards the foot of the bed. A small shape the size of a cat was moving sinuously beneath the tangled covers. As his muscles tensed, he felt it again, warm flesh rubbing against his thigh.

He jerked his leg and yanked back the covers.

It raised its beautiful head and smiled, wetting full lips. Clinging to his thigh with small, powerful limbs, its smooth nakedness squirmed against him as it pulled itself higher yet, a swollen heat pressing lewdly between its belly and Bobby's leg.

Don't move, it whispered in Bobby's mind. Don't move now.

Bobby's breath caught and tears pricked his eyes. As he stared down his chest and belly, they rose and fell, but his muscles seemed locked in position. The only movement was the steady, sensual ascent of the beautiful living puppet.

You want this and you know you want it, it boasted deep in Bobby's mind.

Soft laughter rang in the darkness as its arms grasped the prize it sought, growing louder as the flaccid flesh began to stir. It has a mind of its own, the soft, deep voice taunted. It doesn't need your heart. If it needed your heart, it would take it. Just like it took your head years ago.

…

The dim room and the husky voice of the older boy drifted beyond him, the fading wisps of smoke from half-remembered campfires, and the child that was Michael was deep beneath the covers, warm with sleep. And in that sleep he is sitting on the toilet in his undershirt. He looks between his legs and sees him hanging there, his soldier, a little man with a pink helmet on his head.

"No," says the Toy Soldier, who now is standing on the window sill, sunlight glinting on his thimble helmet. "You've spent too much time with that soldier, Michael. Much too much time." Shaking his head, the Toy Soldier jumps from the window sill to Michael's skinny little boy knee. The Toy Soldier seems taller now. "I've come for your heart," the Toy Soldier says.

…

Brandy can remember it only in vague fragments: Stumbling through the cinders of the deserted parking lot. An impression of traffic speeding by, lights slashing the desolate horizon. The wet wool odor of the Salesman's topcoat as he leaned against him. Thinking of the galoshes and leggings in the cloakroom of Mrs. Salisbury's second grade classroom. The light going on in the pale pink room. The Salesman undressing him.

It was warm in the pale pink room. And rain lashed at the aqua draped window.

Brandy lay on his belly on the big motel bed, wearing only the jockstrap and socks the Salesman had slipped on him. In the bathroom, the water went on. He could hear the Salesman whistling some golden oldie in the shower.

There was a clatter in the cashbox on the nightstand. Responding to the impulses flowing through the thick rubberized cable connecting it to the meter, the bed began to undulate beneath him. A large video screen blinked on. Through an immobile warm water haze, Brandy watched the scene before him take shape.

"Yeah," a young man in a jockstrap and socks said, lying on his belly on an undulating bed identical to the one rocking beneath Brandy. "Massaaage awaaaay . . ." He lit a cigarette and turned his stoned face towards Brandy, licked his lips, and winked. "Try the Midnight Channel," he whispered, disappearing as bright colors shifted and faded.

From a strand of willows smothered in Spanish moss, orchestrated by the swelling sound of an autoharp, the camera tracked through thick clouds of Dry Ice, turning, turning . . .

Brightness slashed through the monochromatic moonlight, spilling from the window of a weathered building at the edge of the swamp. The camera crept closer now, peering through that window:

Light flooded the small room. Black and white tile. Red tub, toilet and lavabowl. Chrome fixtures. Mirrors with tube lighting. A bathroom shrouded in steam.

A handsome young man looked up, laughing in surprise, his water-beaded flesh filling the room, multiplied in the steam misty mirrors, each reflection colliding with another until he becomes a naked legion. His lithe body was bursting with life, a rapidly snatched towel in his right hand barely obscuring his genitals.

Brandy tried to close his eyes. No. It's not possible. Not even a blink. In the old days, the Indians used to cut the lids off the eyes of enemies they had captured. His older brother had told him that. So their enemies would have to see whatever was planned for them. A warm tear slipped from his left eye. It rolled along his cheek and wet the pillow.

Brandy's secret. His brother. Brandy's oldest sister had slipped him a 'lude for his brother's funeral.

"Babe," the young man said, fiddling with the towel like a stripper. "I'm back!"

As Brandy stared into the screen, a patch of steam was clearing on the only mirror that was not filled with the young man's gyrating flesh. In the depths of that mirror, Brandy could see himself reversed, sprawled belly down on the whoreishly rippling bed, the jockstrap and athletic socks somehow more revealing than his nakedness would have been.

In front of his staring reflection, on a black porcelain counter in front of it, a straight razor gleamed.

"Must be the adult channel," the Salesman laughed from the open doorway of the steam shrouded bathroom. Brandy tried to look over his shoulder, but he couldn't lift his head from the pillow.

On the screen, the young man dropped the towel. Naked, he blew Brandy a kiss, one hand stealing lightly around the slowly thickening curve of his sex.

Brandy heard the Salesman moving behind him. "I've got a surprise for you," the Salesman said. Brandy heard a loud, metallic click. "It's in my sample case," the Salesman said.

· · ·

"It means the world to me," the Toy Soldier tells Michael. "You won't miss it. You've never used it. You don't need your heart to play soldier." On Michael's shoulder now, the Toy Soldier whispers in his ear. "Your boatman, Michael. Your boatman and the boy in blue. You never gave them your heart. Nor would you take theirs. But I will take it now, Michael. And with it I will mend the dreams. With a heart I can do so much. And you can wake up in the great light beyond your game of soldiers."

Michael's breath is coming in short, ragged gasps now.

"Choose now, Michael," the Toy Soldier whispers. "The light, Michael?" The Toy Soldier's breath is warm in Michael's ear. "Or more soldiering?"

· · ·

"It's mostly boring things," said the Salesman, sitting on the edge of the bed behind Brandy. "In my sample case? Scalpels, sharp scissors, little metal hammers. Boring things. But there is this, too."

On the television, the young man pressed his jutting erection against the inside of the screen. Between the glass and his firm belly, it looked mashed and bloated, an angry and insistent red.

There was an elastic snapping sound behind Brandy. "Rubber gloves," the Salesman said softly. The rocking bed swayed beneath the Salesman's weight. "Just watch our friend on the screen," the Salesman whispered. Brandy could feel his breath on the naked flesh of his buttocks. The breath was very cold.

Two of the Salesman's gloved fingers, wet with lubricant, slipped between Brandy's cheeks and into his body. "I think you'll like this," the Salesman smiled, his fingers sliding smoothly out. "It's one of my samples."

The young man was pounding on the inside of the screen now.

Between his legs, Brandy felt something large. Cold. Metallic.

"Do you know what a speculum is?" the Salesman asked. "The word itself is actually Latin," he said, sliding the metal cylinder into Brandy. "For mirror? Each of these instruments is especially designed for exposing the interior of a particular body passage or cavity." The Salesman ran a rubber gloved hand between Brandy's legs. "Do you feel exposed?" the Salesman asked. "This particular speculum," the Salesman whispered, "has a special attachment to increase accessibility . . ."

Behind the glass of the television, between the young man's straining legs, the trunk of swollen flesh spasmed, its form shifting, redefining itself from the bloated column of blood and muscle. The plumlike head turned its pouting mouth, flashing white and even teeth, smooth tissue forming a cameo likeness of the ecstatic face of its sweating, moaning host. The leaping shaft had become a rippling torso.

Before Brandy's stunned eyes, as perfectly formed hands began pushing against the pale, blue-veined flesh of the host's groin, hair began to sprout on its small, beautiful head, its heaving torso, a thick patch between its taut nipples, a fainter line along its rippling belly, a darker patch at the point at which it was straining out from the tangled thatch of the host's pubes.

There was a sudden movement in the steam, a gleaming. The screen ran red as it slashed out again and again and the creature hurtled free of the torn flesh, crooning now:

Brandy, it sighed in the center of the pounding that was Brandy's mind. Brandy . . .

"It's time I used this," the Salesman said, stepping to the screen with a little silver hammer. "Aren't you glad I have it?"

As the glass shattered, leaking steam and blood into the pale pink room, Brandy felt it leap against him. A swollen heat at its center, its warm, wet flesh was sliding upwards, moist along the cold tense flesh of Brandy's inner thighs.

. . .

Bobby shivered, pulling his bathrobe more fully around him. He had awakened to the shrill cry of sirens about twenty minutes earlier. He lit a cigarette and watched the wet dawn spread along the streets below.

The city never sleeps, he thought. Isn't that a song? He drew bitter smoke from his cigarette. Motown honkytonked in his head, with a roll of drums. So we meet here in the shadows, while the city sleeps . . .

Behind him in the rumpled sheets, Michael groaned deeply and started.

Bobby turned around. "Good morning," he smiled quietly.

Michael stared at him for a moment, disoriented. He sighed and rolled over. "Shit," he murmured. He had awakened in a cold pool of come.

"I know," Bobby said, looking down at the misty street again. "This isn't the time to say it . . ." Two old men in slickers walked by in the street below, laughing and gesticulating. "But do you remember how much fun we used to have?"

. . .

There was shattered glass everywhere. Firemen, police, two blond ambulance attendants, paramedics, and a milling crowd of the early and unwholesomely curious formed a constantly shifting wall around Brandy where he lay under rough blankets on the wet asphalt.

Two plastic bags on stretchers had already been loaded into a panel van that seemed in no hurry to leave. A revolving light on its white roof threw flashing tendrils of amber on the hulking carcasses of the flattened motorbike and the twisted and smoking remains of a red Volvo.

"Shock," a paramedic said, shining a light into Brandy's staring eyes. "But he's lucky," he said to his partner. "If he'd gotten into the car, he'd be broiled dogmeat like the driver and the kid."

Two cops wandered into the doughnut shop down the street.

A handsome young man with dead eyes leaned against a lamppost on the edge of the crowd, idly rubbing a pale chest and belly framed by a dark, unbuttoned shirt.

V

Rain. *The damp basement of an apartment building. Within the padlocked chicken wire of the tenant storage area, a forgotten cardboard box. Split open. Spilling its contents.*

Pages swollen with the stagnant water that creeps in dark streams over the shattered concrete of the floor, a book lies helpless. Its spine is broken.

A snapshot has been used as a bookmark. A faded Polaroid, edges brown and curling. A young man in bathing trunks is laughing and waving. On the bridge of his sunburned nose is a pair of broken glasses held together with electrician's tape. He is peeping out of the sea of damp pages over halfway through the book, guarding K.C.'s favorite passage.

The old myth.

In this myth, the first being was one. Divided, each half roamed the wasteland, searching for the other. For this, all bodies are cleft with hungry orifices. For this, bodies cling and entwine, convex and concave, struggling to become whole. For this. An anatomy of loneliness.

ANGELS

Kenneth Charles Cooper pauses, out of breath at the corner. He has run all the way up Academy Street from . . .

He ran all the way . . . But it's very dark on Academy Street. It must be very late.

The night makes him feel very small, suddenly. It's like once in science period when he looked through the wrong end of a telescope and everything looked so small and far away. Except that now it's like someone else is looking down through the wrong end of that telescope. Looking right down at him. He feels lost in his Speed King sneakers. It's pitch-dark on Academy Street and the windows on all the houses are staring at him blindly.

Boy, will his mom be mad! Even if this isn't a school night, it's way past his bedtime.

He can't remember if this is a school night or not.

. . .

Two teenaged boys catcalled from a crowded tour bus.

Johnny imagined them dead in some very spooky way. Starved to death in a hidden subbasement. Mutilated corpses dumped without ceremony in a culvert. Snotty noses cut off with garden shears. Genitals missing. Intestines torn by broken glass rods.

It happens, Johnny thought. It's in the papers every day. He smiled vaguely. Careful, kids, he thought.

"Hi," said a young man emerging from the overpriced coffee shop. "Don't I know you from somewhere?"

Johnny hesitated for a moment. The guy was expensively dressed. But he seemed too young and attractive to be a john. Kink, maybe.

"Depends," he said, smiling up engagingly.

...

Now Kenneth Charles Cooper tiptoes up the stairs in the darkened house. Quiet as a shadow, alert as Captain Masters on a commando raid against the wicked Vegetable Men of the dreaded planet Akron, K.C. slips along the hall.

His bedroom door creaks, so he opens it very, very carefully, Speed Kings creeping on the soundless carpet.

Safe! In the dark, he trips over a pile of *Weird Galaxies* magazines and bumps his knee against the footboard of his bed.

There is a deep sigh and a tousled head turns on the rumpled Batman pillows. K.C. stares at the sleep-flushed face in the pale strip of moonlight. A mop of unruly cowlicks. Full lips not quite closed over very slightly bucked teeth. One chipped incisor from a collision with Chuckie Caines' cleats in gym class last year.

K.C. feels very cold and very tired. He's only twelve years old and this is his room and this is his house and this is his town. And there really aren't any such things as those pods that people hide in the garage under tarpaulins.

...

Johnny had feigned indifference to the ride in the Rolls. He had calmly folded the $100 bill into the watch pocket of his jeans and coolly watched the trees move in to surround the twisting highway.

A stone building sprawling on several miles of wooded land. Johnny had smiled, "the Tuesday night jackpot."

"If you don't mind," said the young man after bringing Johnny into an overfurnished pseudo-Edwardian bedroom, "you can undress now. And if you give me your clothes, I'll hang them up for you," he said.

"Whatever you say," Johnny said, slowly unbuttoning his Levi's.

"I don't mean to rush you," the young man said. "But you needn't put on a show for my benefit. I'm being paid for this, too."

"Oh," said Johnny, stepping out of his underpants.

"There are, of course," he smiled, "several rather peculiar details."

Kink, Johnny thought, matching the young man's smile. "Of course," he agreed.

The young man put Johnny's clothing on several padded hangers in the closet. "In the drawer of the nightstand," he smiled. "One of the details."

Opening the drawer, Johnny found a pair of torn boy's briefs.

"They'll probably be a bit too small," the young man said, closing the closet door. "Even for someone of your . . . stature." He smiled. "But the waistband, after all, will stretch. And there really isn't that much else left of them, is there?"

"They're . . ." Johnny's voice caught.

"Food coloring," the young man smiled. "On the practical side, there's another hundred for you in the morning."

Johnny stepped into the torn briefs as the young man opened another drawer.

"Now," the young man sighed. "Lie down on the bed. Yes. That's right. Face down. Perfectly still now. Just close your eyes and listen to the music." The young man gently ruffled Johnny's hair. "It'll put you in the appropriate frame of mind."

Tinkling music crept into the room, repetitious and slightly scratchy. The sort once cheaply recorded on little yellow plastic disks for children to play on their very own little windup machines. Expensive little machines decorated with G clefs and dancing bears. Music for rich rainy afternoons on a toy scattered carpet.

"Wait," Johnny whispered. As he started to get up, the young man pushed him down. The young man was very strong.

"There's only one more thing."

"Listen," Johnny rasped. "I've changed my mind, I . . ."

"Now," the young man smiled, pressing Johnny firmly into the soft mattress. "That isn't very professional, is it?"

And then Johnny felt the prick of the syringe.

As the darkness rushed around him, he heard children's voices singing.

"You better not go in the woods today, it's better to stay at home," the voices sang. "If you go into the woods today, you'd better not go alone . . ."

. . .

A very quiet Kenneth Charles Cooper stands in his darkened bedroom, lost, listening to the steady, even breathing of the child in his bed.

If K.C. pulled back the covers and undid the drawstring on the child's striped pajama bottoms, he knows he would see a small heart-shaped mole on his lower belly, just about two inches below the tan line. K.C. had measured the distance once with a red plastic ruler that had a pencil sharpener on one end of it.

In a few years, that little mole will be hidden by coarse dark curls.

No. He doesn't know that. He doesn't want to know that. It must be time to wake up now. K.C. closes his eyes. But he knows it won't help. The warm tears on his cheek won't help, either.

He sits down at his desk by the window. His Social Studies textbook is lying there, open to page 112. There is a messy pile of notebook paper on the desk, too. And a number 2B Ticonderoga pencil sketch of Captain Masters. It's a pretty good drawing for a kid.

K.C. looks out the window at the pale moon beyond the leaves of the Dutch elm in the backyard. In the corner of his eye, he sees a gleaming. He closes his eyes and he can see a living room. He is standing in front of a sofa and he is very tall. A young man in an unbuttoned flannel shirt and blue jeans is sitting on the sofa. There is a pile of bedding next to him.

"Don't you like me?" the young man asks him, cocking his head and looking up at him. And something else. It makes K.C. think he has to go to the bathroom. But then he realizes that isn't what the feeling is at all. And now K.C. knows. When he leaves this room with its slightly sour smell of sleeping boy, he can never come back. This door is closing.

But there are others.

...

When they had discovered that Brandy had no insurance, they'd sent him home, warning him that he had a mild concussion and should take it easy for a few days.

Even though his head hurt, Brandy had nearly laughed. Insurance.

He had felt torpid and out of sorts for several days, lying in his unmade bed, staring at the sad, framed blonde hanging on the wall. If he'd had a phone, he'd have called someone.

If he had someone to call.

He could have called Michael or Bobby.

"Would you?" he had asked the framed blonde. "If you were me, I mean?"

The blonde didn't answer. She continued to stare off into space, lost in her own frozen dream.

"They don't mind fucking me every once in awhile," he told the blonde. "But I don't think they'd be real excited about holding an ice pack to my head or making me some chicken soup, if you know what I mean."

As he drifted off to sleep again, he thought he heard the blonde laugh. "I thought you'd know what I mean," he mumbled, smiling as his pillows overtook him.

. . .

Cold with sweat, Johnny is lying on the straw-mattressed bed in the back bedroom. The bed that they sleep in. Mommy and her second husband.

His underpants are torn. He ripped them. Mommy's second husband ripped them. Johnny can still smell the whiskey, sweet as vomit in the cramped and stuffy room.

Mommy's second husband had wheezed. And Johnny had heard the fabric rip, had tried to scramble away. Mommy's second husband had pinned him to the bed. Mommy's second husband had panted, sweating in the dark.

His mouth is salty with blood. He has lost a baby tooth. Mommy's second husband had punched him in the mouth when he had screamed.

"Mommy!" he had screamed. "Mommy!"

But Mommy was down at the Junction. Mommy was at the phone company.

If they had a phone and Johnny called the phone company, Mommy would say "number, please."

Mommy said "number, please" all night long at the phone company.

Tommy is crying in the other room.

Mommy's second husband is yelling at Tommy in the other room. Johnny shouldn't have screamed. When he screamed, he woke Tommy up. Mommy's second husband is in Tommy and Johnny's bedroom now. Tommy begins to scream.

Johnny tries to get up. But his arms and legs are made of water. Sore.

Sometimes Mommy talks about parties down at the phone company. "I have your party now," Mommy says at the phone company. "That is a two-party line," Mommy will say.

They have a lot of parties down at the phone company.

"I have your party now," says Mommy at the phone company.

...

Blond again, Brandy turns, naked in tangled sheets, light-years from Hyannisport, far above Van Nuys, swimming up from a dream of sainted knights and dragons. Beside his head, an open telephone.

Bungalow bedroom. Blank white walls. On a dresser, a large handbag with a folded newspaper sticking out of it. Bobby pins, an empty lipstick cylinder, rubber bands, cough tablets, and other small details in a silt of face powder.

A clutter of packages open and unopen. A table lamp with a crooked shade leans drunkenly on the anonymous wall-to-wall carpeting. A pillow has tumbled soundlessly to the floor beside the rumpled bed.

The room looks like someone has just moved in or is in the process of moving out. It could be any of a thousand bedrooms. But it is this one. An AP wirephoto bedroom. Grainy and famous.

"I don't know why," she smiles at him, wrapped in a white terry cloth bathrobe. "But I'm never here anymore." She laughs. "It's been so long since I've been here."

The open phone line shrills its Pacific Bell deet da deet.

"I don't know why," she whispers. "Can you tell me why?"

"Because we needed them," Brandy whispers back, the soft words tumbling in a smear of sunlight.

...

Kenneth Charles Cooper holds onto the idea of Academy Street. Whenever his concentration wavers, he is overwhelmed by infinite space. Overwhelmed by infinite space, K.C. thinks. I am overwhelmed by infinite space.

The only light on the Academy Street he is imaging is at its distant end. A light brighter than the sun. This is my street, he thinks. And that is the light at the end of it.

He thinks about the young man in the unbuttoned flannel shirt. And a gleaming. And a little silver frame.

It's that easy.

From the little silver frame, he stares into the darkened room from inside the glass:

The bedsprings creak. "Johnny," the man in the bed calls softly. He is leaning on one elbow, turned toward a path of light streaming across the hardwood floor. Light spilling from a door that is ajar.

As the young man pulls back the covers, K.C. slips from the snapshot of Academy Street into this lanky adult body. He feels its pulses, its muscles working, its wonder. It's his.

It's that easy.

Beyond the door, someone is crying.

"Johnny," K.C. calls again. His voice now, but deeper.

As he steps through the door, he can see his body everywhere, multiplied on the mirrored walls, each reflection of this tall, strong body colliding with another until he becomes an army of fully grown, perfectly formed K.C.'s.

Flattened against the wall is the small young man who had hovered in the darkness between the pencil sketch and the old Dutch elm and the silver moon. The young man who had smiled and said "Don't you like me?"

He is crouched against the mirrors and tiles now, shivering in his underpants. There is something childlike in his terror.

"Are you okay?" K.C. says softly in the voice that he can hardly believe is his own. He steps forward, marveling at the length of his legs. As he touches the young man, there is a sudden gleaming.

And the perfectly formed flesh he has just slipped into is ruptured now, torn and ruined and rushing with pain.

He slides down. Down, sliding against the mirrors, slipping along the tiles.

And there is fear and anger and sadness and, oh, the pain . . .

And it isn't that easy.

It isn't that easy to give up your flesh like a worn-out coat.

And the child that was K.C. leaks away with the blood and sadness, leaving the anger and the fear and the pain to the ruin that was the adult and that is nothing now but a mouthless shriek.

. . .

"No," Bobby had said. "I'm serious. Really serious."

"But why?" Michael had asked, cracking a beer.

"Why not? You hate your job. It doesn't pay shit. I'm not crazy about mine, either. What? We suddenly have careers, for Christ's sake? We could get jobs anywhere."

"Where?"

"Anywhere," Bobby had sighed.

He sighed again in the darkened room, exhausted and restless, beached on the stubborn shore of Michael's sleep.

Baltimore.

Once, when Baltimore and Bobby and Michael had been new:

Michael at night school. Bobby is bored. Aluminum foil on the rabbit ears of the television.

The laundry calls to him from the closet hamper. Laundromat change jingling in his pockets, Bobby leaves the living room to the television women in miniskirts and plastic go-go boots who race to the beat with bobbed West Hollywood pageboys in turtlenecks and double-knit, manikins ruled by their clothing.

Musky, Michael's underwear and socks. Soiled cotton still softly shaped by the body it has clothed and clung to.

On the television a woman's screams and gunfire: Bobby slipcasts his flesh into Michael's castoffs, a wet plaster prince in clay class . . .

We can wear their clothing, it slips on more easily than their skin. It knows them better than we ever will. It has held them more intimately than we ever can.

Dizzy, with green gym shorts.

A decade later, Bobby gasps, turning his face into the pillow. It smells of Michael's hair.

Where are we going? Bobby asks the dark, his body colliding with Michael's, shivering like steel filings on a magnet, heart pounding, sweating, slippery with tears and semen.

Breathless, Bobby inhales a deep sigh that floats up from Michael's sleep.

. . .

The white light at the end of K.C.'s dream of Academy Street is closer now. The street seems to flicker and fade a spinning second. Think of what is, not what isn't, K.C. whispers soundlessly in the oak lined dark.

For a moment, K.C. is a laughing boy of sixteen in red bathing trunks. Sunlight on swamp water. The salt of sweat. A sweet self-centered ache stirring from belly to chest. Calmer now, he is an old couple in rockers listening to a windup Victrola. A fox trot. An old woman, he hears the scratchy music and thinks of the old Grange Hall in Truxton, a blue silk gown, the old man young in an ill-fitting suit. An old man, he clears his throat, a paperback in his age-freckled hand. ". . . dust. The thunder of horses' hooves echoed in the canyon below. Blackie pulled his . . ." Lighting a cigar, he becomes the smoke and yearns for the light, brighter now.

His death is out there, too painful to touch, lost for now, twenty years of his life held hostage. It hovers in darkness, on the edge of troubled dreams, confused, blind with anger. Waiting. Alone with others.

K.C. pulls back from the light, hungry for a stillborn future, cheated of years of warmth, bereft of bodies that he's clasped.

. . .

The sheets are sweaty. Johnny lies on his stomach in the summer bed.

"Come here, Tommy," he whispers to the dark. "I've got something to show you, Tommy." Hot against his belly. Pressed between him and the sheets.

There is a whimper in the dark.

"Just touch it first," says Johnny, sweating.

"Tommy isn't here," whispers the dark.

"Tommy?" Johnny says to the pillow.

"What a surprise," whispers the dark. "What a surprise we have for you!"

"Surprise," Johnny murmurs, trying to turn over.

"Ready." A whisper from the torn boy's briefs.

The wet elastic waistband holds him fast. "Guess who's here?" it sighs.

· · ·

Bobby trapped in tangled sheets.

The dresser in Baltimore. Michael's drawer. Clean underwear, briefs blazing white as bridal gowns, socks neatly paired. Several sweaters. Jockstrap. Bike. Large. The pouch, slightly unravelled, depersonalized, smelling of laundered rubber.

Beneath a Fordham sweat shirt, a small Boy Scout overnight kit. Bobby unbuckles buckles.

A pair of boy's briefs. J.C. Penney's size 14. The elastic is worn, the pouch yellowish. A pair of red bathing trunks. Size L. A small tear exposes the ragged mesh support lining inside. Wrapped in a folded square of wax paper, a faded snapshot:

Slightly out of focus, edges curled, colors turning. The boy is leaping into the air, dark, wet hair flying round his laughing face, thin, knobby legs suspended above uneven ground. Borrowed red bathing trunks several sizes too large for him slide low on his belly. The flesh is lightly downed and pale there, blue-veined as marble below the tan line.

A folded sheet of notebook paper, blue-lined, three hole punched. Blue as the veins in the boy's lower belly, smudged ink whispers:

"For Michael, on his birthday
Fishing
Canasta
Frog's legs
Swimming
The brass bed at the top of the stairs.
Everything they wouldn't understand.
I love you.
Gabriel
P.S. Please keep this. I know it's silly."

Magic. The dead speak. In Baltimore. Michael's drawer.

...

Michael's dream is a glossy magazine. A sheaf of brochures from West Hollywood. Full color films shot in producer's homes miles above the old motel rooms. Videotaped sighs and whispers.

He shops aimlessly for the bored grace of surfers. The tattooed elegance of metal shop dropouts. Surprise on the faces of boys headed nowhere who have arrived. They have the look of expensive lawns, deeply plowed and endlessly seeded.

Michael pauses. A boy's bedroom. On a nightstand, a bag of peanuts and several empty gum wrappers. A twin bed. A cheap cotton spread, beige with red stripes. On the bed, tensed legs in white cotton athletic socks, knobby knees bent and sprawling wide apart, Gabriel smiles dreamily, eyes closed, back arching, sweatslicked belly pulled in tight, an orgasm flying from his slippery fist.

A half-open door. A second Gabriel stands spying, one hand inside red bathing trunks identical to those that lay in a crumpled heap at the foot of the bed.

"Forever," the conjugating Gabriels whisper on the next page, demonstrating lurid possibilities.

Michael presses forward, but the shiny surface of the page shuts him out.

"You can't touch us," they say tonelessly, joined at the crotch, blue movie

Siamese twins.

"You're old now," the Gabriel on top murmurs. "You can watch."

Hands trembling, Michael turns the page.

Bright as neon, the breakfast nook in his kitchen:

Well oiled, Johnny stands smiling on the table, a sensational advertisement for the famous brand of underwear he is wearing, eyes bright as silver dollars. Kneading the pouch of the briefs, he laughs and stretches out on the table, belly down. He spreads his legs languidly and flexes the deep cleft of his cotton clad buttocks, winking at Michael over one shoulder. "Cute," Johnny sighs. "You think I'm very cute, don't you?"

"Let's improve the view," says the young man in jeans and a bomber jacket.

"Slow," Johnny sighs. "They like it slow. Slow for the older men."

Smiling, the young man clicks open a straight razor. "Watch closely, mister."

The straight razor snags the white cotton at the crotch seam between Johnny's spread-eagled legs, slicing it from where it is pressed between the mound of Johnny's genitals and the table top to its tight elastic waistband. Dead eyes smiling, the young man grasps the material in both hands and rips it open.

"Hungry?" the young man whispers.

"Cut him off a piece," Johnny sighs.

...

Bobby slips past Michael's shallow sigh, sliding out of bed. Bare feet on chilly floorboards, right arm tingling where the weight of Michael's sleeping body had turned a tourniquet. Wind and rain rattle at the windows.

The radiator won't clank again for hours. Bobby shrugs on a wool shirt of Michael's.

Bathroom light chain. Bobby stands on the cold tiles and the full-length mirror sees him. Drawn face floating like smoke above a slim pale strip of torso, framed by black and blue wool.

The linen closet whispers open.

Inside a bottom drawer. Towels. Washcloths. A withered orange studded with cloves. At the bottom of the drawer, an old leather dop kit. Zippered. Unzipped.

A pair of boy's briefs. Calvin Kleins. Size 14. They could be new except for a flaking smear on their pouch, yellowish and musky. Wrapped in a folded square of wax paper, an instamatic secret:

Michael's bed, surprised by the battery driven flash. Sleeping or dead, Johnny has kicked the quilt back on his side of the bed. He is wearing a football jersey, now rumpled up around his hairless chest, and one knee-length striped cotton sock. Between the cotton socked leg and its smooth and naked mate lies the boy's exhausted sex, a blind mollusk abandoned by the tide on an oil slick beach.

A folded square of paper, bits of pad gumming still clinging to one edge.

Bobby crumples it in his left hand.

You can try, mister, whisper the soiled briefs, but we aren't your size.

...

Moving inside him again, but Johnny doesn't care. It's what they always want. Boring. Let them have it. Drugged dentist's office drilling.

Sticky. Damp beneath him. He would laugh if he could catch his breath. He must have come. He didn't even feel it.

If there were a television, he could watch Perry. But there is no television and it's dark in the drawer, folded under underwear and socks, flat as a photograph, surrounded by snapshots. "Hi, K.C.," he tells the pillow. "Nice towel."

"Tommy misses you," the snapshot says softly.

"Tommy," Johnny mumbles.

Oh. A rush of warm wet.

Cold air.

Darkness and a rough blanket cover him.

Cistern sounds.

"Dump him," the voice says. But Johnny doesn't hear it.

Tommy. And the lights.

...

"Well, look who's here," Vivian says to Vernon. She turns around and smiles at Michael in the back seat of the big old Ford. Her left arm is in a cast and sling as it was on the day she died.

Florida shopping centers speed by. "Guess Bobby isn't coming," says Vernon.

"Not everyone's ready," smiles Vivian. "Go ahead, Vernon." She shakes her head. "Vernon is fighting World War II again, Mikie."

"That landing strip in Sicily was the muddiest mess I ever saw. And those Guineas, they'd never seen a flush toilet. Just squatted in the bushes like animals."

"Goes on like that for hours," Vivian says.

"Now, when I got my leave to come back stateside, it was an even bigger mess. Waiting around and waiting around. And that wop heat was something else . . . So I go over to Knaught. Or maybe it was Bedbeck. Can't rightly think which it was. They was both big palookas."

"I was thinking about something else," Vivian says. "When it happened?"

She scratches at the itch inside the cast on her left arm with a Chinese back scratcher. "Picked up this back scratcher down to the Kmart. Handy thing. Had to use a crochet hook before I got this."

"Whichever one it was," says Vernon, "Bedbeck. Knaught. They was both quick to turn a buck . . ."

"I thought maybe you'd want to go out in the boat with Gabriel. Instead of in the car with me and Vernon." She smiles and shakes her head. "Up to you. Either way, it's better than having to go alone."

"Or," says Vernon, "with whatever else might have come when you called the dead." He laughed. "Now, in Sicily, you see . . ."

The Florida light seems to be getting brighter ahead of them.

. . .

The semen haunted underwear in a puddle at his feet, Bobby, on cold tiles. Where has he hidden you? the mirror asks him, a naked ghost, exhausted in an open wool shirt that is far too big. The smile of the scar cut in the coarse hair above the mirror's sex strikes Bobby as very odd. And he wanders closer until his own flesh meets the cold glass, hiding the backwards scar from view. His breath obscures the mirror's face, his reversed twin.

Do you know my name? the mirror whispers, warming its flesh against his.

"Brandy," Bobby sighs. "Your name is Brandy."

. . .

Feverish, Brandy drifts, careless and transient as snow settling on wet blacktop. Shadows shift and slide around the room. An immense shadow on a whitewashed wall, a map of winter cities so changed you'd never know them now. Drowned boys laugh as, in that cold Nebraska room, his older brother dies again. As he always does. His brother is slipping through his fingers again, as he will do nightly, when the streets first claim him.

A bruised sixteen with his older brother's hand growing cold in his. His two pale sisters take turns.

"You've got to sleep," they say. "You've got to eat."

Let them eat. Let them sleep. The body on the bed has never warmed their nights. The body cooling on the bed isn't theirs.

Awake now. Gone. Tired years ago.

Fuck that, Brandy mutters. He ain't coming back. He struggles with the sheets, hoping to rearrange his dreams with several punches of the pillow.

Drifting again, blank with the pain in his head. As if a mirror has found him, he sees a drawn face floating like smoke above a slim pale strip of torso framed by black and blue wool.

It could be his brother. But it's not. His brother was much larger. Four walls of flesh to hide in. It could be me, Brandy thinks. It could almost be me, though.

Living or dead. Living or dead? The faded fleurs-de-lys whisper from the walls.

Dealer's choice, sighs the goddess. The sadness in her eyes is sweet as the fragrance of expensive perfume. Perfume once pressed upon her by those who drained her and left her, a legend in a black-bordered frame.

Oh, Brandy thinks. Oh, Bobby.

...

His own idea of twelve years old, K.C. wanders his dark prayer of Academy Street. The lights at the end of the street are much brighter. So many paths of blinding light now, double and triple crossings.

Misty autumn afternoons, daydreaming through rubber booted boredom, the odor of wet wool. The capitols of Europe. A map of the world. Boundaries to memorize. Preparation for trips never taken. Quiero dos huevos fritos. Je m'appelle Kenneth Charles Cooper.

The old car is on the old road. Too many doors may close too soon. Hovering here, hungry for the light, K.C. has a shriek to swallow and a body to bind, his own suitor now.

I am the quiet, K.C. whispers. I am what you thought you lost. You are what I became. Captain Kansas City Cooper reaches through the dark for the radiant pain.

Lanky legs, big knuckled hands, full lower lip, flesh clothing for lengthened bones. The odor of himself engulfs him as vivid as it was when first discovered on the flesh of others. Sensation tumbles over sensation and child and man slide beyond it, dreaming light.

...

"Another mile to Tin Pan Alley. Any minute now," Vernon says.

"We was on our way to Tin Pan Alley when it happened," Vivian says. "They have this Senior Spaghetti Feed every Thursday. All you can eat."

"Right on schedule," Vernon says as the truck looms over them.

The light is a nova now, and there is a glint of rippling water, the drag of heavy oars, and Gabriel's voice, warm as a whisper. White light. As full or empty as a cathedral of dreams.

...

January follows January as it always has. Perhaps Brandy has followed Bobby. A small flat in Paris between the wars. Perhaps Bobby has followed Brandy. A castle in Spain.

In the small park beside the Church of Old Souls, an army of bruised children leans in the ragged wind, waiting, soundless and unseen, eyes resigned and blank as the ravaged moon, the only witness to their vigil.

One drifts apart, dreaming of keys and snapshots and secret drawers filled with a future long passed. If there are hauntings, they are like this. Children left too long in the cold.